SHOWER OF GOLD

SHOWER OF GOLD

Girls and Women in the Stories of India

Retold by

Uma Krishnaswami

with illustrations by

Maniam Selven

Linnet Books
1999

CHILDRENS ROOM

First published 1999 as a Linnet Book,
an imprint of The Shoe String Press, Inc.,
2 Linsley Street,
North Haven, Connecticut 06473.

Library of Congress Cataloging-in-Publication Data

Krishnaswami, Uma, 1956–
Shower of gold : girls and women in the stories of India / by Uma
Krishnaswami ; with illustrations by Maniam Selven.
        p.   cm.
Summary: A collection of stories featuring strong female figures
from Hindu mythology, Buddhist tales, and others from
the history and folklore of the Indian subcontinent.
Each piece is accompanied by background information.
ISBN 0-208-02484-0 (cloth: library: alk. paper)
1. Women—India—Literary collections. (1.Women—India—Literary
collections.) I. Selven, Maniam, ill. II. Title.
PZ5.K88Sh 1999
891'.1—DC21   98-43142
                                                                 CIP
                                                                  AC

The paper in this publication meets the minimum requirements
of American National Standard for Information Sciences—
Permanence of Paper for Printed Library Materials, ANSI Z39.48-1984. ∞

Designed by Sanna Stanley
Design graphic courtesy of
Himalayan Publications/Hinduism Today
Printed in the United States of America

To my grandmother,
Ponnamma Rangachari,
who taught her daughters
to think for themselves

Contents

Contents

Guide for Teachers and Storytellers

I sit here on this rock
And over my spirit blows
The breath
Of liberty

– Mettika (Buddhist nun, sixth century B.C.)
from the *Therigatha,*
translated by Uma Chakravarti and Kumkum Roy

Introduction: Traveling Tales

When you live in one state, one country, one continent, and then leave it for another, home becomes a place not on the map but in the heart. Of course, you take memories with you. You take old loves, and old griefs and angers. And you take stories. If you are like me, you remember every single one you have ever been told, and they travel with you, just like your toothbrush or your clothes. Also, when you leave a place for a long time, you can never quite go back. Even if you do return, both you and the place have changed while you've been gone. So the stories you took with you are often a very important link with the place you left behind.

Stories also move through time. In very many communities in my native country of India, more people cremate their dead than bury them. So there are no gravestones, no church records, to help people learn about those who went before them. But there are stories, and they travel long after those who first told them are gone.

The stories in this collection come from varied sources. A number of them are tales I heard while I was growing up in India. Versions of many of them can also be found in other parts of the region called South Asia, or the Indian subcontinent. This includes the present day countries of Bangladesh, Bhutan, India, Nepal, Pakistan,and Sri Lanka. The high plateau land of Tibet is often included as well. Although it is closer to Central Asia, its art and culture have many links with the subcontinent.

Many of the stories in this book are from Hindu mythology.

SHOWER OF GOLD

Hinduism is the oldest continuously practiced faith in the world. It is so old that no one really knows when it began, and it has no single founder. Hindu mythology holds many mysterious, magical characters, some of whom appear in the stories in this book. They include gods, or *devas*; demons, or *rakshasas* and *asuras*; and people of all sorts—queens and kings, holy men called *rishis*, and women and men both wise and foolish. The stories often make a point, or teach a lesson. Since beliefs, worship, and folklore vary with place and time, all Hindu people are not alike, and so of course, neither are their stories.

Three of the stories here are Buddhist tales. Buddhism was founded by the Prince Siddhartha, who was born in the sixth century B.C., in what is now the Indian state of Bihar. The prince grew up in luxury, but yearned to break free of his sheltered existence. He sought to understand the meaning of suffering and pain in life. Leaving his palace, he wandered across the land, seeking this truth through questioning, prayer and meditation. Later in his life, he became known as the Buddha, or "the Enlightened One."

The Buddha taught that a middle way of moderation helps all souls find the path to truth. Buddhist stories often include people giving up riches to follow the Buddha, just as he himself left a royal life to find enlightenment. Buddhism, and Buddhist stories, spread from India to southeast Asia, and as far as Japan and China. Buddhism is now practiced less in India than in other parts of South Asia such as Sri Lanka, Bhutan, and Tibet.

In the stories in this book, you will find some ideas occurring again and again. One that comes up in both Hindu and Buddhist stories is reincarnation. This is the idea that after death souls are reborn, literally, into new bodies, and live many lives in order to gain wisdom. In the story, "Gotami and the Mustard Seed," Gotami decides to seek knowledge and master it. Only in another life does she actually achieve this goal. Just as Gotami is born again, so is the Buddha. In fact, Buddhist tradition includes tales called *Jataka* stories, which are accounts of the Buddha's previous lives.

Buddhist stories also contain another important idea—that the cause of suffering is attachment to earthly things. Many Buddhist tales carry the message that if you see this world as only a temporary part of the soul's bigger journey, it is easier to achieve the ultimate goal of being enlightened or finding the true meaning of all life.

Other stories in the Indian subcontinent do not come from religious traditions, but from very old literary works. One of the most famous of these is called the *Panchatantra*. It is a magical maze of stories-within-stories, one of the earliest books of fables anywhere in the world. It was possibly written as long ago as the second century B.C., although the original work is long lost. Translations of it into Arabic are thought to have inspired later works, including the fourteenth-century English poet Geoffrey Chaucer's *Canterbury Tales*; and several versions of the stories translated into European languages in the eighteenth and nineteeth centuries, that we know today as *The Thousand and One Nights*. Although "The Magic Tree" is sometimes viewed as a story from the *Panchatantra*, it might actually have been a later addition to the original frame tales.

Still other stories are from oral folk traditions, and were often told by women. Some, like "The Goddess and the Girl," are grounded in Hindu tradition. Others pit harried daughters-in-law against mean-tempered mothers-in-law. In these stories, a weakling husband often colludes with his mother to torment his wife. Sometimes, as in "The Daughter-in-Law Who Got Her Way," the daughter-in-law wins out.

Some stories here are from neither mythology nor folklore, but from the place between history and story that we call legend. "The Warrior Queen of Jhansi," "The Love Story of Roopmati and Baz Bahadur," and "Vishnu's Bride" are based on the lives of real women. When oral tradition is strong, we are often left confused about where history ends and story begins. In some ways, it may not be important to ask, "Is this story real?" Perhaps more meaningful questions might be, "What does it tell us?" or "What feelings are expressed in it?"

Since stories, like me, have a habit of traveling, I've included in this collection some that travel well, and some that are special to me. So in this book I don't presume to represent all the women and girls of the Indian subcontinent. I couldn't possibly do that. I've tried instead to offer glimpses of their images, and snatches of some of their stories. Each is followed by a note on background and source. The glossary, pronunciation guide, and character list in the back might also help thread a path through the stories.

Girls and Women
in the Stories of India

Stories, of course, are reflections of life, and of the hopes, fears, and dreams of the people who live it. The women and girls in these stories reflect different times and conditions. Their tales are sometimes about struggles to achieve the right to make their own decisions, control their own lives. Often this is in settings where men hold the power. Yet even here we find stories of strong and determined women —and we find goddesses with magical powers.

Goddesses in Hindu mythology are sometimes the companions of the gods, but with their own special abilities and strengths. Sometimes they are gentle and nurturing, sometimes strong and fierce.

Saraswati is the companion goddess of Brahma, the creator of the universe. She has the rather wonderful role of the goddess of learning. Reading, writing, and music are held to be her sacred arts. If you speak eloquently or sing well, Saraswati is said to "live on your tongue."

Lakshmi, the goddess of wealth, is often portrayed with the god Vishnu, who preserves order and balance in the universe. Lakshmi sits on a lotus flower, sometimes flanked by two elephants with their trunks raised in salutation. In both "Sita's Story," and "Vishnu's Bride," the adoption of a baby girl is seen as good for the house, because it is like inviting Lakshmi in. As it turns out, in both these stories, the baby girl is in fact Lakshmi herself in human form. Some say the goddess chose to come to earth as Sita, to help rid the world of evil, and as Andal to show the power and beauty of love.

SHOWER OF GOLD

The god Shiva holds the powers of destruction and dances the dance that ends each cycle of creation. His role is crucial to the balance of life in the universe. His companion goddess, like so many of the gods and goddesses in Hindu stories, takes many forms, and is known by many names. Sometimes she is gentle and nurturing, as Parvati the mother, or Uma the bride-to-be. Sometimes, as Durga, who protects the world from evil, or Kali, the vengeful mother, she is terrible and fearsome, and deals death to evildoers.

Some scholars have speculated that the worship of a great, all-powerful goddess is a very ancient tradition in South Asia, going back to a time even earlier than Hinduism. Whether or not that is true, there are Hindus today who are quite likely, when thinking of divine power, to see that power as female. In many households, the *devi*, or goddess (as either Lakshmi, Saraswati, or Parvati, in any one of their varied forms), is worshipped before any of the gods.

The goddesses associated with gods such as Shiva and Vishnu are sometimes described as their wives, but their relationship with the gods goes far beyond this role. Sometimes the goddesses are described as the *shakti*, or strength, of the gods, who would be powerless without them. Sometimes they are their consorts, or companions. Sometimes the male god takes female form. In one tale, Vishnu appears as a dancing girl to make sure the demons do not get a share of the nectar of immortality churned up from the ocean of milk. In another story, Shiva and Parvati combine to form a figure which is half-male, half-female, and therefore possesses unlimited energy and power.

The idea of learning as sacred, and as female, goes back a very long way in the Hindu tradition. In the *Vedas*, the most ancient of Hindu texts, speech itself is thought to be a goddess. Her name is Vak.

Girls and Women in India

The most holy of chants in the Hindu faith, called the *Gayatri mantra*, is considered to be female. Of the elements of Hindu prayer ritual—fire, earth, and water—only fire is a male god. The earth, called Bhoomi, or sometimes Bhoodevi, is a goddess. She is sometimes seen as a form of Lakshmi.

All water in Hindu traditions is thought to represent the river goddess Ganga. In many parts of India, it is considered bad luck to name a river after a male god. Of the major rivers of the country, only the Krishna and the Brahmaputra have male names. Some people say that the Brahmaputra is an angry river, and floods so often, because it is male.

An interesting twentieth-century variation of goddess worship is the depiction of India, the country itself, as a goddess—*Bharat Mata*, or Mother India. This is a tradition apparently invented by leaders of the nineteenth century social and political movements resisting British rule over India. It might have been inspired by an anti-British novel published in 1882 by a writer named Bankim Chandra Chatterjee. This book portrayed India as a mother goddess, and true patriots as her children, combining European ideas of nationhood and progress with ancient images of the goddess. One scholar has dubbed this "matriotism."

Some people wonder why, when goddesses in Hindu mythology play such magical and powerful roles, Hindu society has not given women more power. The birth of a son is still greatly desired, as in the story, "The Goddess and the Girl." Girls in the subcontinent have higher rates of infant mortality and illiteracy than boys, indicating that they are perhaps not taken care of as well as boys. Some historians think that women held greater power three to four thousand years ago, but that as society changed, power shifted into the hands of men. Others say that there never was a "golden age," and that women have always had to struggle to find justice in the societies of the subcontinent, much as they have all over the world.

In our century, four of the countries of this region (India, Pakistan, Sri Lanka, and Bangladesh) can boast of current or recent female heads of state. While individual women are obviously able to rise to positions of great power, however, many women still endure injustice and discrimination. Today, women's groups throughout the region are becoming stronger, and voicing their concerns more loudly and insistently. But old practices die hard in traditional societies, and marriage, divorce and inheritance laws in most countries of the region continue to discriminate against women.

The stories in this book inform us that the struggle of women to be heard is an old one. The web of tales called the *Ramayana* is perhaps the most beloved of Hindu stories. It is one of the two great epics of Hindu mythology, the other being the *Mahabharata*. There are stories in this book drawn from both of them. The *Ramayana* is most often told as the journey of the hero prince, Rama. Yet hundreds of renderings of this tale exist all over India and Nepal, and in countries as far away as Thailand and Cambodia. Among them are songs and stories, documented both in the northern town of Mithila, home of the princess Sita, and in the southern Indian state of Andhra Pradesh. These "other" versions tell the tale from Sita's point of view, and offer a female perspective on a traditionally male-dominated story.

In early Buddhist thought, women were regarded as incapable of setting aside material needs and wants. Marriage and motherhood, the main social roles of the women of these far-off times, seemed to promote earthly attachments, and therefore got in the way of realizing enlightenment. Women were often suspected of placing temptation in the paths of men seeking the truth through religious or monastic life. Yet in many Buddhist tales, we also see women trying to find a place in that life.

Today, it might seen odd that people, including women, would want to leave their daily lives to follow the Buddha on a path that offered few physical comforts. One answer is that entering the *sangha*, or holy order, released some women from the drudgery of housework, or unhappy marriages, or the difficult life of a widow. For men, too, the religious order often brought freedom—from hard work in the fields of rich landowners. For the queens in the story, "The Buddha and the Five Hundred Queens," it seems more a matter of equality. The kings became the Buddha's disciples, so the queens also wanted the privilege of being admitted to holy orders. After all, in our time, comparable questions have been raised in the Western world, in the matter of women being ordained as ministers in some Christian denominations, or enlisting in military service.

In Indian history, the notion of women fighting on the battlefield is not a new one. Between the eleventh and nineteenth centuries A.D., there were some remarkable queens who governed kingdoms, battled enemies, and earned the loyalty and love of their subjects. Among the Muslim monarchs who ruled in what is now Pakistan and northern India, Sultana Razia earned her place in history when she came to the throne in the eleventh century. It is said that she dressed "like a king," much to the dismay of the society of the time. She also issued coins in her name, and led her forces into battle.

There are records of other queens of the region who were famous for their skill as rulers, or their valor on the battlefield. But Lakshmibai, who ruled the central Indian kingdom of Jhansi in the nineteenth century, is the one who best embodies this image of the warrior queen. Her story, "The Warrior Queen of Jhansi," is the tale of a historic heroine whose fame grew to legendary proportions. Movies have been made in India about her life, and she has been compared to Joan of Arc. Popular songs still celebrate her heroism.

From Sita to Lakshmibai, from the goddess Durga to the child Supriya, the women and girls in this story collection offer us images from a vast geographical region occupied by diverse groups of people. How women are known, thought about, and valued is reflected in these characters. Their voices sing of strength and mercy. Some are compassionate, some loving. Some are defiant, others brave. Their stories are as rich as the shower of gold from which this book draws its title.

The Goddess
and the Girl

Now listen, now listen. Once a man and his wife were traveling the path that leads to the cave of the goddess called Vaishno Devi. Although this man and his wife had a dear little daughter, they were unhappy that they did not instead have a son. "We will ask the goddess to bless us with a son," they said, as they set out on their pilgrimage.

Now their little daughter came with the man and his wife on their pilgrimage, to see the shrine of the goddess, and to be in her presence. The way was steep. Sometimes the little girl got tired, and her parents had to carry her. Then she felt stronger, and she could walk again. Because she was a small child, she played as she walked, and sometimes, as she played, she laughed out loud. Whenever they reached flat places in the climb, she drew a quick little grid in the dirt, and played hopscotch with small, round stones. She pushed rocks off the edge of the path. Then she leaned over as far as she could, giggling to see them bounce and tumble down the mountain slope.

"Don't waste time," the man said to his daughter. "We have a long way to go yet, and then we have to go all the way inside the cave. If we're too late, they won't let us in."

"Don't lean over," the woman scolded the child. "You'll fall down the mountain, and then what will we do?"

11

"Hurry, hurry," the father urged. "Do you think we're the only ones going to see the goddess today? There'll be hundreds of people waiting in line. Maybe we won't even get into the cave. Hurry, hurry!"

And on they went, slower than the father wished. Hundreds of other pilgrims pushed past them, calling out, "Everybody say it! *Jai Mata Di!* Victory to the Mother!"

"She has hair black like smoke, the goddess," said one pilgrim to another.

"And she rides a lion," replied the first, as they pressed on.

"Did you hear that?" the mother asked the little girl. But the child was too busy playing to pay much attention.

"Say it in the front! *Jai Mata Di!*"

"Say it in the back! *Jai Mata Di!*"

"Old people, young people, everybody shout it! *Jai Mata Di!*"

Now the little girl jumped up and down, shouting *"Jai Mata Di!"* in a small, shrill voice, right along with everyone else.

Suddenly, the very thing the mother had feared happened. The child missed her footing, and tumbled down the mountain side.

"O Mother Goddess! *Vaishno Mata!*" cried the woman. "Come back, child! Where are you?"

But there was no reply. The little girl had rolled off the steep shoulder, down the rocky slopes, and was out of sight. The woman gave a great wail, "My child, my child is lost! Help, someone help us!"

"Stupid woman, be quiet!" hissed her husband. "Now we'll never get to see the cave of the goddess."

But the woman sobbed, "We came to ask for another child, and now the one we already have is lost. I will not leave here, until we find her. I don't care if there are a thousand people waiting to see the goddess. I want my daughter back."

The Goddess and the Girl

The mother and father searched the hillside. They pushed into the forests, tearing their clothes, bloodying their hands on thorns and brambles. Their search seemed hopeless. The woman's face was wet with her tears. Suddenly, they came upon a clearing in the trees, where the sunlight dappled the ground, and butterflies fluttered their busy wings.

There was the child. She sat, quite cheerfully, on a fallen tree trunk, munching on handfuls of roasted nuts and dried fruit.

"How did you get here?" cried her parents. And her mother cried, "My poor child. You must have been so afraid, all alone in the jungle."

"I wasn't alone," said the little girl. "I tumbled down. Oh, that was frightening. But there was a girl here, and she helped me feel brave again."

"Girl? What girl?" asked the parents.

"Oh, that girl—where did she go?" and the child looked all around her, searching for someone who had been there only moments before. "She was bigger than me, but not as big as you, mother. She kept me company. And she healed my scratches. She told me stories, and she gave me all kinds of good things to eat."

"What did she look like?" said the father slowly. "This girl."

"Oh, she was beautiful," answered the child. "Her hair was black like smoke. She wore red clothes, and she carried shiny things in her hands. Oh, and she rode on a big, yellow dog."

The husband and wife looked at each other. "Goddess! Vaishno Devi!" they exclaimed. Tears in their eyes, they hugged their daughter, forgetting all about the son they had come on this pilgrimage to get.

The parents understood. "Who needs a son?" cried the mother. "We have our daughter. Let us all go now to the shrine of the goddess and give thanks to her for saving our blessed girl. *Jai Mata Di!* Victory to the Mother!"

The Goddess and the Girl

For the parents knew that the goddess in this place always takes the form of a maiden with flowing black hair. And it is said she comes on the back of an enormous, tawny lion.

Notes on
The Goddess and the Girl

Even though it may not seem so at first, the goddess in this tale is kind and merciful. Clearly, she watches over careless little girls. I first encountered this miracle tale in 1976, on a trek with my parents to the cave of the goddess Vaishno Devi, in the hills of the northern Indian region called Jammu, in the state of Jammu and Kashmir. Traditions related to the worship of Vishnu and Shiva are said to meet in the ceremonies honoring this goddess. The path to her cave is long and steep. At the end of it one must enter the cave, and then crawl through a ninety-foot tunnel, to emerge into the sacred space of the goddess. Rounding a corner on the way up, slightly dizzy from the exercise, we rested. Near us, an old woman half-sang, half-told, stories to her little group of fellow travelers, and anyone else who cared to listen. Our understanding of Dogri, the language she spoke, was limited, and it has been many years since I heard this, so any distortions to the tale are my fault entirely.

Kathleen M. Erndl refers to this story of Vaishno Devi in her book, *Victory to the Mother: The Hindu Goddess of Northwest India in Myth, Ritual and Symbol* (New York: Oxford University Press, 1993).

Savitri and the
God of Death

There was once a king whose greatest sorrow was that he had no child. He kindled a sacred fire, and prayed to the goddess Savitri. Soon, the goddess appeared out of the flames, her face as golden as the fire.

"O goddess, grant me sons," begged the king, "for it is said that sons will bring blessings to my soul."

The goddess replied, "No sons, O king, lie in your future. No sons, but a daughter, whose like has never been seen upon this earth. A daughter shall be yours, and she will be the blessing of your old age. She will be wise, graceful, loving, and strong. Her fame shall spread throughout the land."

And the king bowed to the goddess Savitri, and was happy.

In time the king's favorite queen bore into this world a baby girl with radiant face and clear, bright eyes. On the tenth day of the baby's life, the day on which children must be named, the queen exclaimed, "What a shining child she is! Let us call her Savitri, in honor of the goddess who blessed us with her."

Savitri grew into a bright and beautiful young woman. So sparkling was her wit and so radiant her bearing that the people said, "This princess brings light to the world."

But there was one problem. When Savitri grew to be the age for marriage, and the king and queen set about looking for a husband for her, there were no suitors. Young men were afraid of her intelligence and her spirit. "Marry Savitri?" they said. "Why would any prince marry a princess wiser, more learned, more clever, than himself?"

So the king said to Savitri, "They are afraid of you, my child, because they are not good enough for you. So you must choose for yourself. Go out into the world, my daughter, and find yourself a husband worthy of you."

The princess agreed. She left the court with maids and servants in attendance, to seek a worthy husband.

The king was worried that his wise and witty daughter might never find a husband good enough for her. He invited to his court the sage Narada, who roams the three worlds carrying messages—some say, telling tales. "What do you think, O Narada?" asked the king. "Will she ever find anyone fit to be her husband?"

Narada stroked his long white beard, and strummed upon his instrument, the *tanpura,* which he always carried with him. It is the drone of instruments, and if you have ever heard one, you will know that it repeats its notes against all others, over and over. Some people say Narada carried news from place to place, like the *tanpura* repeats its notes.

Before Narada could answer the king's question, Savitri returned.

"My daughter!" cried the king. "I see from your smile that you have been successful. Tell us who the lucky man is. Which kingdom is he heir to, what lands does he rule?"

"My father," said the princess. "Not in a mansion, but in a forest, did I find my prince. His parents are a king and queen, old and blind, whose enemies have taken their kingdom and robbed them of everything they owned. But they are kind and gracious. It is their son, Satyavan, I wish to marry."

SHOWER OF GOLD

Narada turned pale. He thrummed his *tanpura* in agitation. "Princess, you are making a sad mistake," said he. "Satyavan is kind and kingly, intelligent and talented. But this I know—he will be dead in a year's time. Your daughter, O king, will be a widow."

The king's face clouded with fear. "Child, if this is true it is sad indeed. Can you not find another prince?"

"Father," replied the princess, "my heart has chosen. I will marry no one else."

So the king, forced to agree, rode into the forest with many of his courtiers. They bore gifts and flowers for the old king and queen, the parents of the prince Satyavan.

"Noble and gentle people," said Savitri's father to the young man's parents. "I come to ask if you will bless the wedding of my daughter to your only son."

Satyavan's parents protested, "The princess Savitri is used to the ways of the court. How will she live in the forest with us?"

But the princess replied, "I care nothing for the luxuries of court. With Satyavan by my side, the trees of the forest will seem richer than any canopy of silk."

When it was clear that nothing would change Savitri's mind, and that Satyavan was set on marrying her, both sets of parents had to agree to the wedding. Narada himself was priest at the ceremony, and blessed the couple as they took the seven sacred steps around the fire.

After the wedding, Narada took Savitri aside, "Princess, let me teach you a chant, a *mantra.* Repeat it continuously for the three days and three nights before the day your husband's life is to end. It will give you the power to see what others cannot." And Narada left to spread the word of Savitri's marriage to Satyavan.

Savitri and the God of Death

The newly wedded prince and princess soon went to live in the forest with the old blind king and queen. Seeing his daughter go, the king mourned at the thought of the hard life she would have, and the sorrow that awaited her at the end of one short year. But his queen said, "Look at her face. She's so happy. That's all that matters."

Savitri and Satyavan lived a life of simple joy in the forest. They chopped wood for cooking fires, and ate berries, nuts, and wild fruits. They delighted in each other's company, and Satyavan's old parents said, "Truly, this princess has brought light into all of our lives." But as the year rolled by, the shadow of Narada's words grew ever larger, and soon it loomed ahead.

Satyavan, of course, knew nothing of Narada's prediction, and said to his wife, "Why do you watch me like that? Why do you look so sad?"

Savitri only shook her head and smiled to hide her sorrow.

As the year drew to its end, and Satyavan's last day of life grew close, Savitri prayed and fasted. For three days she ate nothing, and for all those days and the nights between them, she repeated the magical chant that Narada had taught her a year before.

The dreaded morning dawned, crisp and clear. Satyavan, as usual, went out with an axe to fetch wood. Quickly, quietly, Savitri slipped out of their hut and joined him.

"I will come with you," said Savitri to Satyavan.

"What, to fetch wood?" he asked, laughing.

Savitri smiled back at him, clasping her hands to stop their trembling.

Satyavan found a huge banyan tree, which looked like a hundred trees, with all its hanging rootlets. He climbed onto one of its branches, and began chopping at another. Suddenly he stopped and mopped his brow. "I feel so tired!" he exclaimed. "I need to rest a while." And before he could climb down, Satyavan lost his balance and crashed to the ground.

"My husband!" cried Savitri.

Satyavan's eyes were closed. He seemed deep in slumber. Savitri sat beside him, cradling his head.

Immediately there appeared before the princess a being splendid and dark as rain clouds. It was Yama, the god of death. He was fierce, with eyes red like blood. He rode a water buffalo. In his hands was a noose to catch the spirit of Satyavan, who lay with his head in Savitri's lap, his life ebbing slowly away.

Now those who are mortal do not usually see Yama until the time their own deaths draw near. But Narada's *mantra*, which Savitri had learned and used, made her see the dark one in all his glory.

"Move aside, princess," said Yama, his voice ringing through the green forest. "Your prayer allows you to see me, but you must know it is dangerous to play with Death. Away—I have come for your husband's spirit." And Yama cast his noose over Satyavan's body. He snared Satyavan's bright spirit and bound it tightly, leaving his body cooling and lifeless. Then Yama rode off on his water buffalo.

Savitri jumped up, and ran after the god of death.

"Not now, princess, it is not your time," said Yama harshly to her.

"Then give him back to me," replied Savitri.

"I cannot," Yama responded. "Return. Cremate your husband's body. Cast his ashes upon the river. Mourn him as a loving wife should."

But still Savitri followed Yama.

"When I married Satyavan," she said, "I promised to be with him always."

Savitri and the God of Death

"You cannot come to the dark lands of the dead," said Yama. "And I cannot return your husband's life. Ask for anything else, princess."

"Well, then," said Savitri, "restore good health to my husband's parents. Make them see again."

"You are compassionate as well as loving. It is done," said Yama. But still Savitri followed him. He led her through thickets of thorns. Her feet bled, but still she followed Death.

"Go home, princess," said Yama, but Savitri replied. "I must be with my husband."

"Not that, princess. Ask for anything but that."

"Very well," said Savitri. "Give my parents many more children."

"Given," said Yama, with a flash of red eyes. "Now go back."

"What is the use," asked Savitri, "of granting all my wishes if you take away my happiness?"

"I see you are both brave and determined," said Yama. "I cannot give you back your husband, but I will grant you one last wish. Only do not ask for your husband's life."

"Well then, Lord Yama," said Savitri, "grant that I, Satyavan's loving wife, may bear a hundred sons."

"Granted!" Yama swung around on his water buffalo and faced Savitri. "Now, turn back, princess, and leave your husband to his fate."

Savitri smiled. "Lord Yama," she reminded him gently. "I am Satyavan's wife, loving and true. The only children I will ever have must also be his. And if they are to be mine and Satyavan's, I really must have him back, mustn't I?"

Yama stopped cold, and lowered his noose. He gave the smallest of nods. His mouth curled in a smile. And Yama, Lord of Death, said to Savitri, "Truly, princess, I must acknowledge defeat at your hands.

Return to Satyavan's body, and he shall regain his life. He shall live for four centuries, and you shall rule at his side."

And so it happened. Savitri went back to where her husband lay. She watched as Satyavan awoke, as if from a deep sleep. Warm was the welcome they received when they returned to the kingdom of Satyavan's parents. As for the old blind king and queen, their joy knew no bounds when they found that they could see again, and their old bent backs grew straight with new youth.

Savitri's parents rejoiced when they learned how their daughter had saved her husband, and brought vision, health, and kingdom back to his parents. When the time came for Savitri and Satyavan to rule, they united the two kingdoms, and governed them in peace and prosperity.

Notes on
Savitri and the God of Death

Savitri's tale is part of the story mazes that make up the *Mahabharata,* often referred to as one of the two great epics of Hindu mythology and literature (the other is the *Ramayana*). The story of this clever heroine takes on magical proportions when it is told to young girls struggling to understand both the emotional tangles of adulthood and the mysteries of life and death. In some ways, Savitri is the perfect wife, loyal and loving. Unlike Hindu wives in other stories, however, she is not submissive.

In her article on the Savitri story, narrative scholar Lee-Ellen

Savitri and the God of Death

Marvin tells of Asha Bhide, a storyteller of Pune, India, who offers an interesting and unusual interpretation. In it, the banyan tree from which Satyavan falls is the human body. Savitri is human nature. So when she asks for good health and eyesight for her parents-in-law, she really means, "Let me have the vision to see what is true or divine." When she asks for a hundred sons, she really asks that her soul progress through a hundred lives. In this way her story is transformed into a spiritual quest, with many layers of meaning. See "Two Contemporary Performances of Savitri in Pune, India" by Lee-Ellen Marvin in *Traditional Storytelling Today: An International Sourcebook* edited by Margaret Read MacDonald (Chicago: Fitzroy Dearborn, 1998).

My mother-in-law, Hema Krishnaswamy, helped me by clarifying the sequence of events in this tale, which I had heard as a child, and later read in various retellings. The story of Savitri is also retold in *Myths of the Hindus and Buddhists*, by Ananda K. Coomaraswamy and Sister Nivedita (New York: Dover Publications, 1967).

The Buddha and the
Five Hundred Queens

Many years ago, a royal prince left his palace and roamed the land in search of truth. When he discovered it, people called him the Buddha, "the enlightened one." He taught about peace, and compassion, and whenever he spoke of these things, people listened. The more he talked, to groups big and small, in towns and cities and villages across the land, the larger grew the numbers of his followers.

Once the Buddha stopped a war, using only wise words for his weapons. After this, five hundred kings who had been about to fight each other joined him and became his disciples. "We will leave our wives and our families, and everything we own," they swore, "and we'll follow with you, O Buddha, the path to enlightenment."

Now these kings left behind their five hundred queens, in palaces of marble and gold. At first the queens protested, and pleaded with their husbands to come home. They sent messengers to the places where the Buddha and his followers camped, begging the kings to reconsider.

"Your subjects need you, sire!" cried one of the messengers.

"Who will teach your sons the arts of ruling?" asked another.

But the kings refused. "We follow one who is greater than kings," they replied.

Then Queen Maya, the mother of the Buddha himself, spoke to the five hundred sorrowful queens. She told them of the great work

The Buddha and the 500 Queens

being done by the Buddha. "He is a great soul," she told the queens, "and I must forget that he is my son. Now I am his follower, like the thousands of others who hear him and find meaning in their lives."

"Your husbands search for a path that will free all humankind," said Queen Pajapati, the second wife of the king who was the Buddha's father. "Do not grieve for them. If they can become true followers of the Buddha, the truths that they learn will shine upon all people, for generations to come."

Hearing the words of the Buddha's mother and stepmother, one of the five hundred queens said, "Wise ladies, your words move me. Why should my royal husband be the only one to seek this truth? I too will abandon my robes of silk, and follow the Buddha."

Then another of the queens cried, "I have no need of my gold and pearls. I will come too."

"And I!" exclaimed a third. "My pillows of velvet stifle me now. Let me give them up to seek this path of truth."

"It is not an easy road," warned Queen Maya. "You have much that you will need to give up. The rewards are great, but they are not rewards of this world."

The first queen to speak out replied, "Why should only our husbands be allowed to find the road to enlightenment? We too are willing to seek this truth."

"And seek it we can," added the second.

"Show us how, Queen Maya," said the third queen. "Lead the way, Queen Pajapati."

So the queens sent a messenger to the Buddha. The messenger said, "Lord Buddha, these queens, like their royal husbands, wish to follow you. They want to tread your Noble Eightfold Path, and be admitted to the holy order of your followers."

SHOWER OF GOLD

To the great surprise and disappointment of the queens, the Buddha returned word to them, saying, "Noble ladies, the order is not for women. The hardships are too great. You could not stand the rough lives that my followers endure. Besides, people would gossip. They would say that our order is weak indeed, to admit women."

Three times the queens requested to be accepted to the holy order. Three times the Buddha refused.

"We must take firmer steps," said Queen Pajapati

"Listen," said Queen Maya, "for I have a plan."

And the two queens, mother and stepmother to the Buddha himself, sent word to the other five hundred.

From far and near, the five hundred queens hurried from their palaces. Tasks left half done, conversations dropped mid-sentence, they threw together what they needed for their journey. Soon they were all gathered in the marble courtyard of Queen Maya's palace.

"Are you sure," asked Queen Pajapati, "that this is what you wish to do?"

"We are sure," replied five hundred voices, strong and clear.

"Then take sharp knives," said Queen Maya, "and cut off your beautiful hair, so you will no longer be bound by vanity."

One queen took the jewels out of her hair, and let it fall down her back. Then another followed, and another. They took knives and swords, and cut off their long tresses and braids, until the palace was strewn with the sad remains of once beautiful, raven black locks.

"Are you still sure?" asked Queen Pajapati.

"We are sure, noble lady," replied the five hundred queens.

"Then take off your robes of satin and silk," said Queen Pajapati. "Take off your finery and put on these rough robes, so you will not be shackled by comfort and luxury."

SHOWER OF GOLD

Then the queens stripped off their soft, rich silk clothes, with threads of gold and silver. They put on garments of rough cloth, rags of coarse cotton.

"Here are some begging bowls," said Queen Maya. "These will be your only possessions, so you will not be bound by earthly belongings."

Each queen took in her hand a begging bowl. Now she would depend on the charity of others for her living.

And the queens Maya and Pajapati, too, cut off their hair, and wore rough clothes, and picked up the small wooden bowls that would be theirs. Then together the queens set out to find the Buddha.

They walked for many miles, for many days and nights. They walked until the stones of the road bruised their tender feet, and the thorns of the field scratched their bodies. The sun beat down upon their heads. Many fainted in the heat, and were revived by the care of the others.

So these gentle queens, so used to the comforts of their fine palaces, journeyed on in wind and rain and blazing heat, until finally they caught up with the Buddha and his followers.

"Royal ladies," said the Buddha to the queens. "What brings you here? And why are you dressed this way?"

"We have traveled a long road to see you, Lord Buddha," said Pajapati, bowing. "And you can see, we have proved we can survive the hardships of the road. Now will you allow us to enter your order?"

Still the Buddha refused, saying, "The monastic life is not for women."

Then Ananda, the Buddha's beloved disciple, spoke up, "Lord, I must ask this question. If women are admitted to the order, could they follow the path of truth, and find release from the desires and suffering of the world?"

The Buddha and the 500 Queens

The Buddha, looking at the five hundred queens, saw the determination in their eyes, their tattered robes. He saw their once-tender bodies, hardened by the wind and dirt of the road. He had to reply, "Buddhas were not born on this earth only for the sake of men."

"So then why not admit them?" asked Ananda. And the women who had been queens, Maya and Pajapati and the five hundred, waited in patient confidence for the Buddha's answer.

Finally, the Buddha said, "I have no answer. I cannot refuse. The time has come for women to join the faithful in holy orders."

And the queens, rejoicing, were accepted by the Buddha as his disciples. They became the first order of Buddhist nuns, the beginning of a long tradition that exists even today. They traveled throughout the land, scorning earthly possessions, and bringing to people the truths of the Buddha's teaching. The Buddha and the Five Hundred Queens

Notes on
The Buddha and the Five Hundred Queens

The tradition of women monastics or nuns in Buddhism died out in India in the centuries following the life of the Buddha, but took hold in other parts of the region. In Sri Lanka, there are orders of Buddhist nuns to this day. And when the Tibetan spiritual leader, the Dalai Lama, fled his homeland in 1959 following the Chinese invasion, thousands of nuns were among those who went into exile with him.

Historians tell us that although the Buddha admitted women to holy orders, they were not treated as the equals of the male monks.

For example, they were not allowed to challenge the teachings of the men. Still, getting in was a beginning—and that was hard enough! This story of the Buddha and the queens, as well as the tale in which the Buddha stopped the war among the five hundred kings, can be found in *Myths of the Hindus and Buddhists* by Ananda K. Coomaraswamy and Sister Nivedita (New York: Dover Publications, 1967).

The Daughter-in-Law
Who Got Her Way

Once there was a wife whose husband and mother-in-law both treated her very badly. They beat her. They yelled at her. They made her work very hard—fetching water and cooking, scrubbing, polishing, and mopping. And worst of all, they did not give her enough to eat.

Now in that family's little garden grew a gourd, a plant with squash-like fruit. In week after week of the growing season, this plant bore the most delicious gourds for miles around. The daughter-in-law watered the plant. She picked the gourds. She chopped them and steamed them and fried them in sesame oil. She garnished them with grated coconut and spices and delicious fried mustard seeds, and served them up to her husband and his mother. Every time she did this, the husband and his mother ate the delicious vegetable, and left for her the most measly, weasely, stingy little portion of it. The poor woman had to watch them eat it all. What they left for her was only just enough to make her mouth water, and her stomach growl with hunger.

For a very long time the woman put up with this, but inside her anger simmered like a slow cooking fire. She sat awhile thinking things over, until finally she had a plan. She said to her mother-in-law, "Dear *Amma*, you know Big Aunt, your father's sister?"

"Big Aunt? Big Aunt? Of course I do," snapped the mother-in-law. "What about her?"

31

"Well, I met her husband in the marketplace this morning," said the woman, making it up as she went along, "and he said that Big Aunt is very sick, and she's asking for you."

"What? Big Aunt sick? Why didn't you tell me before, stupid?" And the mother-in-law thrust a ladle into the woman's hands, saying, "I must go at once. Here, you finish cooking this. It'll keep you from being lazy." And the mother-in-law left quickly.

Looking into the pot, the daughter-in-law saw bubbling, boiling, mouth-watering, spiced stew, made with her favorite gourd. "Aha!" exclaimed the woman. "Finally, here's my chance to get a good meal."

The daughter-in-law finished cooking the stew. She checked it for salt and spices. When it was just perfect, she took it off the fire, and let it cool a bit. "Now," said she. "I'm going to take this where I can eat it in peace and quiet."

The daughter-in-law took the stew, cooking pot and all, out of the house, down the street, around a corner, through a big stone arch, and into the grounds of the temple of the goddess Kali. It was the middle of the day. The temple was quite empty. The woman carried the stew all the way inside, until she was in the presence of the stone image of Kali herself. There, sitting on a stone step, she ate it all, as fast as she could, hardly able to wait to taste every last delectable drop.

All the time the daughter-in-law ate, she had of course been watched by the stone image of the goddess Kali. The goddess, amazed by the speed with which the stew disappeared, gasped and put her stone hand up to her own mouth in astonishment. And there her hand stayed.

Now the daughter-in-law noticed the hand of the statue move, but she was so busy eating her stew that she paid no attention. At last her stomach was pleasantly full. She took the pot to the river, washed it out, filled it with water, and hauled it back home.

When the daughter-in-law got home, she was met by her husband's mother, who immediately began shouting at her, "You greedy pig. You cooked up a story to get me out of the house so you could eat my stew, didn't you?" And the mother-in-law beat her about the head with a broom.

Meanwhile the town was buzzing with the news of the statue of Kali whose hand had moved up to her mouth and whose face now wore a look of permanent astonishment. The rumors flew about. In no time at all, they reached the house of the woman, her husband, and her mother-in-law.

Dodging a blow, the woman said, "Oh, mother dear, if you will stop beating me a moment, I can go fix the goddess."

"You? What will you do?" But the mother-in-law, tired, put her broom down and said, "Oh, go away. You've troubled me enough for one day."

The daughter-in-law picked up the broom and went directly to the temple. She said to the priests, "Out! I need to be alone with the goddess." Taken aback at her tone of authority, the priests obeyed.

"All right," said the daughter-in-law to the goddess. "You stood by and watched while they treated me like dirt all these years. Now do something useful for once. Take your hand off your mouth."

The statue of Kali remained still, the look of wonder frozen on her face. The daughter-in-law hoisted her broom and said, "Take your hand off your mouth, goddess, or I'll whack you with my broom."

Slowly the statue of Kali lowered her hand. There might have been a little smile on her face that had not been there earlier, but otherwise she looked just as she had, before the daughter-in-law had gobbled up the stew.

"Thank you," said the daughter-in-law. She went out and said to the priests and the gathered crowd, "You can go see. I fixed the goddess."

Then the daughter-in-law went back home and said, "You can go see. I fixed the goddess."

The husband and his mother ran to the temple. They talked to the astounded priests. They heard the murmurs of the crowd. They exchanged glances of amazement. The mother-in-law opened her mouth to say something, then closed it again. The pair of them, mother and son, came home in silence.

The husband said to his wife, "Er—wife, are you well? Here, sit down and rest yourself."

The mother-in-law exclaimed, "Sweet girl, forgive me my ignorance! I had no idea you were so powerful. And so kind and wise. Beautiful, too. Truly, my son is blessed. Come, sit with me. Would you like some freshly pressed sugar cane juice?"

From that time on, the husband and his mother made sure they were kind and respectful to the daughter-in-law. They asked her opinion on matters of importance. They waited on her every need. And they always, always made sure she had enough to eat.

The Daughter-In-Law Who Got Her Way

Notes on
The Daughter-in-Law Who Got Her Way

This is a tale of a kind that scholars have described as women-centered. It is featured in the now classic collection, *Folktales from India: A Selection of Oral Tales from Twenty-two Languages* selected and retold by A.K. Ramanujan (New York: Pantheon, 1988). In this tale the daughter-in-law is abused until she cannot stand it any more. It is this desperation that seems to give her the power to change her circumstances. In order to make the point of the tale without confusing the reader, I have adapted the story somewhat, leaving out secondary events that build on the initial victory of wits won by the heroine. In "The Clever Daughter-in-Law," a story in Ramanujan's book, after the incident at the Kali temple, the daughter-in-law foils attempts on her life by her husband and his mother, and returns triumphant. She scares them into submission by making them believe she has defeated the lord of death, Yama himself.

When I shared this story with my mother-in-law, she told me of other versions of it, including one featuring the elephant-headed god, Ganesha.

The Mother
of Karaikkal

In a town called Karaikkal in
the south of what is now India, there once
lived a young woman, married to a merchant. Business was good. The
couple lived prosperous lives, and wanted for nothing.

Now the young woman was a worshipper of the god Shiva, whose
dance ends each cycle of creation. She would often go to the stone
temple of Shiva in town and offer flowers at the shrine, and mark her
forehead with holy ash. Sometimes she would slip into the world of
her own thoughts. Then she would dream about Shiva's mighty
dance, about his destruction of the world, and the great cycle of life
of which it is a part. "And how lucky I am," said the woman, "to be a
tiny part of that cycle."

One day, the young woman's husband sent a servant home with a
small bag. "Lady," said the servant, "Your husband, my master, sends
you these. They are the first of the season. He wishes you to serve
them when he comes home for his evening meal." And from the bag,
the servant brought out two mangoes. They were small, as early mangoes are, but ripe and ready to eat.

The young woman's mind was still on Shiva's dance and the
mysteries of the universe. She took the fruit from the servant, and
went inside.

Just then there came another knock at the door. Opening it, the woman saw an old man, wrinkled and bent, his body smeared with ashes. With trembling hand, he held out a begging bowl, saying, "Your charity, noble lady. A hundred blessings on you. Help to feed this old body."

Without thinking, the woman took one of the mangoes sent by her husband and put it in the old man's begging bowl, saying, "Shiva's blessing be with you, grandfather."

Later, when her husband came home, the woman cut the remaining fruit and offered it to him at the time of their evening meal. The husband said, "Why don't you bring the other mango out, too? Then there will be enough for us both."

The woman went into the kitchen to get the other mango. Of course, she could not find it. Confused, she suddenly remembered that she had given it away. She was embarrassed, and exclaimed, "O Shiva! What have you done to my mind? What will I tell him? That I gave away the fruit, but couldn't remember it?"

Suddenly, in her hand, as if put there by someone present but unseen, there appeared a mango, warm and ripe and golden. The woman, startled, said to herself, "Well, it's a mango, at any rate." She cut it up, and took it to her husband.

The husband, eating a piece of the fruit, exclaimed at once, "This is not the mango I sent home! Wife, this is no earthly fruit. Even the king's garden cannot grow a mango like this. Where did you get it?"

"From Shiva," the woman confessed, looking unhappily at the ground. "I am sorry. I gave the other one away."

Her husband burst into laughter. "From Shiva!" he cried. "Do you really expect me to believe that? Come on, tell me honestly, where did you get this fruit?"

When his wife insisted that Shiva had given her the mango, the husband flew into a rage. "How dare you lie to me," he shouted. "All right, show me! Ask your Shiva to give you another mango, right here and now."

The woman closed her eyes, and opened her hand. She focused with all the strength of her mind on the god of the dance, Shiva, who lives among the cold high mountain clouds, who dances with ghosts and goblins, who rattles the sacred drum. As she opened her eyes, there, in the palm of her outstretched hand, appeared another golden mango, a perfect fruit, smooth and beautiful. When the husband reached out for it, the mango disappeared.

Now it was the husband's turn to be confused. "W-wife!" he stammered. "You must be a saint. How can I live with you and be your husband, when you have magical powers that I don't understand?" And the husband bowed to his wife, saying, "I am honored to be in your presence, but now I must leave you. You are no ordinary woman."

The husband left, mumbling thanks and apology, amazement and regret, all in one breath. He left his wife, and sailed away to a distant land, lapped by the waves of a foreign sea.

All alone, the woman prayed to Shiva. She said, "I was a wife, and now I am not. Help me."

Suddenly the room grew hot. The woman trembled as the great god Shiva appeared, dancing in a ring of fire. "What do you want of me?" he asked.

Said the woman, "Lord, others fear you, but your presence fills me with joy. I am alone in the world. Let me be your servant, and compose poetry in praise of you."

"Very well," said Shiva. "And what else?"

Said the woman, "I have no need of my youth, this smooth skin, this long, black hair. They only get in my way. Transform my body.

The Mother of Karaikkal

Make it crooked and old. Change my face into one that people will see as ugly. Then release me from the cycle of repeated births, so I can be truly free."

And Shiva, lord of the cycle of destruction, laughed. "So it shall be. You will be so old, *Amma,* that those who see you will call you the Mother of Karaikkal. They will see you as ugly and bent. But your words will be powerful. People will hear them and honor you through many centuries."

At once, the woman's back grew hunched. She became thin, so thin her ribs showed. Her face withered into ancientness. Flowers rained down on her twisted frame, and music filled the air. And the woman was happy.

The Mother of Karaikkal sang many verses in praise of Shiva. She sang of fearsome things, of the ghosts and ghouls that sometimes keep Shiva company, and the terrors and fears that accompany the force of destruction. But she sang also of the brightness of Shiva's truth; of how he once swallowed poison to save the universe, and it made his throat forever blue; and of the goddess Parvati who reigns with him in the snows of their mountain home.

Notes on
The Mother of Karaikkal

Karaikkal Ammaiyar, or the Mother of Karaikkal, lived in the eighth century A.D. She is one of the earliest saints in the Hindu tradition known as bhakti. Some of the *bhakti* saints worshipped Vishnu, and some worshipped Shiva. Their songs and poems, many of which are recited or sung to this day, portray gods as familiar and loved, sometimes awe-inspiring, but never distant. These writers broke with tradition by composing in the commonly spoken languages of their region, rather than in Sanskrit, which (much like Latin in Europe) had so far been the language of worship. A number of the *bhakti* poets were women. Perhaps this is because a religious life was one option open to women who did not want to take on traditional roles of wife and mother.

Statues of Shiva dancing sometimes show a withered old woman with a smile on her face, sitting at his feet. This is the Mother of Karaikkal. Of the many Tamil saints who sang about Shiva, she is the only one whose image has been found far away, in Cambodian ruins of Hindu temples. Some say that Cambodia is where her husband fled, taking with him the story of his wife who became a saint. There he married again, and raised a family. When stories of the Mother's wanderings reached him, he retold them to people in his new home, and that is why her likeness in stone can be seen in those far-off temples.

Vidya Dehejia discusses the legend and poetry of the Mother of Karaikkal in *Slaves of the Lord: The Path of the Tamil Saints* (New Delhi: Munshiram Manoharlal, 1988).

The Goddess
and the Buffalo Demon

Long ago, in the time of the first fires of sacrifice, there was a greedy demon, an asura. He had magical powers, and could take many shapes. Most often, he took the form of a water buffalo, so people called him Mahisha, or "buffalo." His hunger for power was so great that he wanted to rule all creation.

"The worlds will be mine, all three," proclaimed Mahisha. "I will fast and meditate, and my power will grow. Gods, demons, and people will all worship me."

So Mahisha prayed for many days and nights to Brahma the creator. Finally, Brahma could no longer resist the might of his medi- tation. "Enough," said Brahma to the asura. "The white heat of your mind will wither the flowers in the gardens of the gods. Ask what you will."

"I seek immortality," said Mahisha. "Make me live forever."

Brahma said, "That I cannot. Life forever belongs only to the gods. Ask anything else, and it shall be granted."

Mahisha thought for awhile. Then he said, "Well, then, Lord Brahma, grant that I shall live forever, or else meet my death at the hands of a woman."

Brahma said sadly, "*Asura*, you might as well ask for immortality. For how could a mere woman defeat one as powerful as you?"

SHOWER OF GOLD

"You promised, Lord Brahma," said the *asura.* "Only a woman can end my life." Brahma had to agree.

Mahisha's power grew and grew. He plowed a path of destruction through the valleys and forests, cities and deserts, of the world of people. He started fires that burned for days. He threw manure upon places made holy for worship. He ripped whole forests out of the ground and threw them into the ocean. Satisfied with the damage he had done to people, he turned his attention to the world of the *devas,* or gods.

Mahisha's armies attacked the world of the *devas.* Routing the *devas* in battle, the buffalo demon ascended the throne of Indra himself, king of the gods. "From now on, no one," proclaimed Mahisha, "shall worship Brahma, or Vishnu, or Shiva. I am supreme in all the worlds." And he sent his spies throughout the lands of people. Wherever there was prayer to any but himself, it was stopped most brutally, and the worshippers tormented and killed.

Finally, the people on earth could stand it no longer. They sent a delegation to the snowy mountain where Shiva lived, and where the gods had already assembled. "Enough!" cried the people. "You must help us. Mahisha is killing good people everywhere. Soon all that is good will be destroyed, and only evil will survive!"

"But he is immortal," protested the *devas.* "There is nothing we can do."

Brahma said slowly, "There is one possibility. . . ." And he explained that a woman, and only a woman, could end the life of the buffalo demon.

"Then that woman," said Shiva, "must do so. And an extraordinary woman she will have to be."

So Vishnu and Shiva, and Brahma too, focused the power of their anger and the energy of their hope, while the people and the *devas* waited anxiously. All at once, out of the combined force of the Three, leaping flames arose. They fused together as if a giant mountain of fire had taken over the sky. From the flames came a mighty goddess, and her name was Durga. She was brilliant and beautiful. Hard anger was in her eyes, and strength was in her thousand arms. She laughed out loud, and her laugh sent an eerie warning echoing through all the worlds.

"You come from the beginning of all the worlds, Durga," said Vishnu. "Yours is the power of the universe . . ."

". . . the source of all its strength," continued Shiva.

"Destroy this demon," finished Brahma, "or he will destroy all that is good."

Then the gods all gave magic weapons to Durga, to hold in her thousand hands. From Shiva she got a trident, from Vishnu a round discus, edged with flames. Indra the king gave her a thunderbolt. And Himavaan the ancient, king of the mountains, gave her a lion to be her steed.

Mounted on her lion and armed with the weapons of the gods, Durga roared a mighty roar, making the tides run from the ocean's shore to hide in its depths. The earth shook in fear. Far away in the kingdom he had stolen from the gods, Mahisha the buffalo demon stopped a moment, feeling a small dread creep into his heart.

Soon Durga's terrible laughter sounded just outside Indra's palace, within whose golden walls Mahisha now lived. He went out to look. For a moment, his eyes were dazzled by the goddess, her hair like a black flag waving in the wind. Anger glittered in her eyes. Her lion roared and bared its teeth, and even the powerful *asura* stopped in his tracks.

"What do you want, woman?" he said roughly. "Who are you?"

"I am Durga," replied the goddess, "and I have come for you."

"For me?" scoffed Mahisha. "What can you do to me? I have powers beyond compare. The gods shudder at my name."

"I am only a woman," said Durga, drawing her trident slowly, "and it is for your life that I am here."

Then Mahisha remembered Brahma's promise to him—eternal life, unless it was cut short by a woman. "Guards!" he bellowed. A thousand asuras rushed out to protect their master.

Alone against the thousand, Durga fought for hours, her thousand arms flashing, her weapons as swift as thought. The battle was fierce and bloody, and soon the *asura* army lay scattered lifeless all around, like broken tree limbs after a storm has spent itself.

Now Mahisha was face to face with the goddess who was to be his doom. Swiftly he changed shapes. First he was a buffalo, snorting and stamping the ground, charging at the goddess with his great horns lowered. But Durga's trident was swift, and the buffalo could not avoid its thrusts. So Mahisha turned himself into a lion. His eyes were red with fury, his claws raked the earth as he sprang. But Durga's own lion steed roared a challenge, and met him with slash and thrust that sent him reeling back.

In desperation Mahisha changed and changed again. He became a master swordsman, then a rogue elephant, then again a buffalo.

With lightning speed, the goddess leaped from her lion. With her trident, she pinned Mahisha to the ground, and quickly ended his life.

"Only a woman," said the goddess, as flowers rained down from the heavens, and the stars danced dizzily in the evening sky. The world reeled with joy at the end of the evil buffalo demon. "But killed

by me, you need not live again. Go now Mahisha, and all you *asura* warriors. Your spirits can join with the spirit of the universe."

Durga returned to Shiva's icy mountain home. "If you need me, ever again," she said, "I shall come back." And as a red gold fireball engulfed the sky, Durga disappeared. In our time or a future one, if evil overtakes the world again, some say she will keep her promise and come back.

Notes on
The Goddess and the Buffalo Demon

In the story of Durga and the buffalo demon, found in the part of the Hindu scriptures called the *Puranas,* (literally, "old" or "ancient"), the demon is said to symbolize ignorance, hatred, and other forces of evil. Durga is the form the goddess takes to protect people from these dangerous negative forces. I have no recollection of having actually heard this story, but since it seems as if I have always known it, the hearing of it must belong to a time quite early in my childhood. The worship of Durga, and of Kali the vengeful, bloodthirsty killer of demons, is common all over India, but most of all in the eastern Indian state of Bengal. Many forms of the goddess are celebrated as well in the northwest, in the foothills of the Himalaya mountains.

Kathleen M. Erndl refers to this story of Durga in her book, *Victory to the Mother: The Hindu Goddess of Northwest India in Myth, Ritual and Symbol* (New York: Oxford University Press, 1993). It is mentioned as well in Tracy Pintchman's *The Rise of the Goddess in the Hindu Tradition* (Albany: SUNY Press, 1994).

Gotami and the Mustard Seed

Cycles of births and deaths, it is said, are like a great wheel turning. In one such turn of the wheel, to parents with little wealth and even less hope, was born the girl child, Gotami. In one of her previous lives, Gotami had been the daughter of a king. She had heard the Buddha of that time speaking of truth. Listening, she had said to herself then, "In one life or another, I too will be learned. I will be wise, and know the truth. I will be blessed."

In this life, which was a poor one, Gotami was a small child, and sometimes sickly. She had wide, dark eyes in a thin little face. When she walked by, the rich merchants and their fat wives spat in the street, saying, "There she goes, a nobody's daughter!"

Gotami listened, but said nothing.

When Gotami grew to be a woman, her parents arranged a marriage for her, with a young man from another poor family. Now, when she walked by, the rich merchants whispered to their jewelled wives, "There she goes, a nobody's wife." Still, Gotami listened, but said nothing.

With the turn of another year, Gotami gave birth to a son. Her parents and her husband and his parents all rejoiced.

"A son!" exclaimed Gotami's father. "Finally, a grandson who can perform my funeral rites, and speed my soul toward its final peace. Daughter, you are blessed to be the mother of a son."

"A son," said her husband's father, "is a gift from the gods." Now Gotami smiled, and her eyes danced in her thin face.

When Gotami walked in the street with her baby held to her heart, the wives prodded their merchant husbands with fat, ringed fingers, and hissed, "Now she's a nobody's mother." But Gotami tossed her head and walked right by them, with her son held proudly in her arms.

Another year turned. Then, one rainy season, a dreadful epidemic of disease swept the village. Cries of pain and suffering filled the air. Death stalked the streets, and found many people. Among them was Gotami's son.

Gotami's grief was terrible. "He is dead, daughter," said her father. "There is nothing you can do."

But Gotami picked up her small child's body, and would not put it down. She went from street corner to temple square, looking for the medicine to cure her son of death. The rich merchants shrank from her in fear. Their wives waved chili peppers in the air to ward off the anger in Gotami's eyes.

"Wife, stop this madness," said Gotami's husband to her. "Let us put our child to rest." But Gotami would not listen.

Finally, someone said, "Sister, the Buddha himself, the enlightened soul, is visiting our town. He holds the key to truth. He speaks of release from suffering. Surely he can help you."

Gotami cradled her dead child, and took him to the Buddha.

"Medicine, Lord Buddha," she said, and in her dark eyes were fear, and anger, and something more. "I seek medicine to heal my child."

The Buddha replied, "Grieving soul, do as I tell you. Go to every house in the village. When you find a household in which no one has ever died, fetch me, from that house, a little mustard seed.

Gotami and the Mustard Seed

"Mustard seed?" said Gotami.

"Mustard seed," replied the Buddha. "Do as I say. Your child will be safe here with me."

So Gotami laid her child's body at the Buddha's feet. She went down the street, and knocked on the first door. "Kind lady," she said to the woman who opened it, "has anyone ever died in your household? If your answer is no, will you spare me a little mustard seed?"

The woman shook her head. "My father-in-law died last year. It was time. He was ill. But I cannot help you."

Gotami knocked on the second door. "Alas, I grieve with you. The fever took my sister, only last week," said the man who peered out through the upstairs window.

"I'm sorry," said Gotami, and she went on.

At the third house, they had lost a grandparent two rains ago. From the fourth, a fall from a tree had claimed the woodcutter husband. The fifth household, too, had been touched by death.

At the sixth house, the man who opened the door said, "Sister, this is an old house. It has known death more times than I can count." And Gotami paused, and walked slowly on.

At the seventh house, Gotami raised her hand to knock at the door. Then she stopped herself. Deep in thought, she came back to where the Buddha waited.

"Do you have the mustard seed?" asked the Buddha.

Gotami replied, "Lord Buddha, the little mustard seed has done its work. I have no need of it. My heart is now at peace."

Gotami laid her child to rest. She said to his spirit, "Forgive me. I tried to hold on to you, when you were no longer mine. Such love is no different from greed. Now I know that all life must end. My child, I must let your spirit go free from the bondage of my love."

And as she left the graveyard, Gotami chanted:

> *"This is the Law not only for villages or towns–*
> *Not for one family is this the Law,*
> *For all the wide worlds both of men and gods,*
> *This is the Law—that all must pass away!"*

Cycles of births and deaths, it is said, are like a great wheel turning. Gotami spent the rest of her life learning the truths of the Buddha's teaching. By the time her end came, she was a great and learned soul. She was a blessed one, named by the Buddha as the first among the wearers of rough cloth—just as she had wished to be, many lifetimes ago.

Notes on

Gotami and the Mustard Seed

This Buddhist tale is an example of the stories told to convey the spiritual superiority of Buddhism over Hinduism. The Buddha and those who followed him saw traditional Hindu practices as full of needless ritual that only got in the way of people seeking the truth. In the story, Gotami is despised because she is poor. Even within her family she is only respected when she bears a son. Before she becomes a follower of the Buddha, her status, or lack of it, comes entirely from her position as a daughter, wife, and mother. Yet in the Buddha's eyes she is capable of great learning, which she eventually achieves. Note that the Buddha himself had to be persuaded that women could in fact participate in religious life—see *The Buddha and the Five Hundred Queens*. Reincarnation is also a theme in this story.

An article in a journal written over 100 years ago details a variant of this tale that is found in the Buddhist texts called the *Dhammapada* (Mabel Bode, "Women Leaders of the Buddhist Reformation," in the *Journal of the Royal Asiatic Society of Great Britain and Ireland*, 1893: 793-96).

Sita's Story

To the king Janaka of Mithila came a gift. In a freshly plowed field, cradled in a furrow of rich soil newly turned, he found a little baby girl. "Daughter of the earth," he said to the bright child. "After the place I found you, I will call you Sita, which means 'furrow.' " He took the baby home to his palace, and raised her as his own daughter.

"What a lovely baby girl!" marvelled the people. "Adopting her is like inviting Lakshmi, goddess of wealth, into the kingdom. Wherever this little one goes she brings light, just as the goddess herself does."

Now in one of the many rooms in that palace there was a mighty bow, which the god Shiva had once given to Janaka. It was so heavy that no one could even lift it, let alone string it or use it to shoot an arrow. So there it sat, gathering dust. Once, when Sita was a young child, she ran laughing through the palace, pulling the king by the hand. When she saw the bow, she asked, "What's that?"

"That," began the king, "is the bow that Shiva gave to me, when—" Then the king stopped in astonishment, because little Sita casually picked up the bow, lifted it high in the air, and then put it back with a laugh.

"Indeed," marvelled the king, "you are no ordinary child. You have the beauty of the earth, and also her strength."

Sita's Story

When the princess Sita grew old enough to marry, the king said to her, "How shall we find a prince good enough for you, golden child?"

The king mused a while. Then he cried, "I have it! In childhood you lifted the giant bow as if it were a toy. Brave men have struggled with that bow. The prince who can string it will marry you." And the king set about preparing for a gathering of princes from far and near, saying, "Only he who can heft great Shiva's bow is worthy of my daughter's hand in marriage."

Meanwhile, news came to Sita of a prince named Rama, in the nearby kingdom of Ayodhya. "Gentle and brave, he is, princess," said the ladies of the court, "noble and handsome, with skin as dusky as twilight." And Sita prayed to the goddess Earth, saying, "Give this noble prince the will to come to the gathering. Grant him the strength to string the mighty bow."

Just as Sita heard of Rama's princely manner and gentle heart, rumors of Sita's grace and wisdom drifted to Ayodhya, and reached the prince Rama as he set out for the gathering.

On the day of Sita's choosing, the bow lay in splendor in Janaka's marbled palace. It took a cart with eight wheels pushed by fifty men to move it into place. Prince after prince, strong and skilled, with smooth limbs and muscles of iron, failed to move the bow. Then it was Rama's turn.

Rama stooped to lift the mighty weapon. He raised it carelessly, as if it were a mere toy. He strung it with such energy that the great bow bent, and snapped in two. Flowers rained from the heavens, and the assembled kings and princes cheered. Sita was overjoyed. She slipped a garland of flowers around Rama's neck, murmuring "Thank you, Mother Earth."

After a wedding that was to live in song and story for thousands of years, Sita went to live in Rama's kingdom. People in both their lands rejoiced.

But as in so many stories of love, sadness came to Sita and Rama. A jealous queen, Rama's stepmother, wanted the throne for her own son. She made King Dasharatha, Rama's father, exile the prince to the forest, for fourteen years. Rama said, "My dearest wife, let me go alone. How will you live in the forest, a delicate princess like you?"

Sita replied, "I married you to be at your side, always. Where you go, I will go too. What you endure, I will endure."

And Rama's brother Lakshmana said, "I will come too, my brother." To cries of grief from the people of the kingdom of Ayodhya, Rama, Sita, and Lakshmana left the palace for the forest, where the trees would be their shelter, and wild berries and roots their food.

The years that followed were at first happy. But sorrow was not far away. For Ravana, a powerful *rakshasa*, or demon, ruler of the far-away island of Lanka, had heard of Sita's great beauty. Ravana was fearsome. He had ten heads. His strength was known in the three worlds. And reports of Sita's loveliness drove him mad with longing to have her for himself.

Ravana sent his uncle Maricha, in the form of a golden deer, to Sita's jungle home. The deer danced through the trees, and Sita was enchanted.

"A golden deer!" she exclaimed. "Husband, can't we have this lovely animal as a pet?"

So Rama followed the deer. It led him deep into the jungle, further and further away from the little hut where Sita and Lakshmana waited. When Rama did not appear, Lakshmana prepared to go in search of him. "I sense trickery," Lakshmana warned Sita. "Be careful while I'm gone. Talk to no one."

Sita's Story

Meanwhile, the demon Ravana came to the hut in the guise of an old beggar, bowl outstretched, asking for charity. When Sita, forgetting Lakshmana's warning, brought food for his begging bowl, Ravana suddenly assumed his own fierce ten-headed form. Snatching Sita from the hut, he forced her into his magic chariot.

Sita struggled, but the chariot ascended swiftly into the air, and began the journey back to Lanka. She cried out for help, to no avail. Desperate to leave a trail, she ripped off her jewelry and flung it to the ground. But Ravana took her all the way to his island home, and only the animals and birds heard her cries. When Rama and Lakshmana returned, Sita was gone.

Rama's grief was frantic. He looked everywhere for Sita. The great vulture king Jatayu, old and frail as he was, had tried to stop Ravana's chariot. Now he lay dying in the forest, wounded by Ravana's sword. "Prince," whispered the wise old bird, "the lady Sita has been stolen away. You will find her in faraway Lanka, Ravana's captive. I heard her screams and tried to help her. For my pains I have paid with my life." Rama's eyes filled with tears as old Jatayu breathed his last.

An army of monkeys and bears came to help Rama and Lakshmana. Together they built a land-bridge across the watery straits that divided the mainland from the island of Lanka. Even the little squirrels carried small pebbles and grasses to hasten the project along. Some people say the stripes upon the backs of Indian squirrels are the marks left by Rama's fingers as he stroked them gently in thanks for their help.

When the army finally crossed the bridge and marched upon the jewelled city of Lanka, a great battle ensued. The clash of swords was so loud it rang through the three worlds. All living creatures watched and waited.

SHOWER OF GOLD

Finally, after all the grief and despair that comes with war, after bloodshed and wasted lives on both sides, Ravana was defeated. Sita was once more reunited with her husband. Their fourteen years of exile in the forest were over. Together with Lakshmana, they returned to their kingdom of Ayodhya.

Happiness should now have replaced sorrow in the lives of Rama and Sita. But the old king, burdened with guilt, unable to bear the separation from his beloved sons and daughter-in-law, had died of grief. So Rama was crowned king, and he wore his crown with a heavy heart.

To make matters worse, rumors began to spread about Sita. Rama should not have listened, but he did.

"Perhaps," said the gossips, "Sita was not kidnapped. Perhaps she went willingly."

"Maybe our king is a fool," said others, "and does not know that his wife actually loved a demon."

"Perhaps, though the demon Ravana is dead, she loves him still."

And so it went on, until doubts began to creep into the mind of Rama himself. Finally, he broke down and said to Sita, "Perhaps it is true. Maybe they are right. While I fought in battle to defeat the evil demon, you lived in luxury in his palaces. You ate and drank, and perhaps you were happy there. How can I take you back as my wife?"

Sita said, "My husband, how can you doubt me like this? You speak as if I were a stranger. It was for you I went to the forest. Is it my fault I was snatched away from you?"

But Rama's eyes were stony. In a voice filled with hardness, he said, "Prove yourself to me. If you speak the truth, then walk through fire to prove it." And he ordered a fire to be kindled.

Servants averted their eyes from Rama as they brought in

armloads of firewood. They stacked the wood. They fanned the flames into life. They obeyed their king at this terrible time, but they wept for their lovely queen.

"Lord Rama!" exclaimed his brothers. "Do not do this. Can you not see how sad your harsh words make our gentle queen?"

The gods came and pleaded with Rama, "Do not do this to her."

But as the flames crackled and rose higher, Sita said, "I speak the truth. Agni himself, the god of fire, will see that I am right." With sorrow and anger in her eyes, Sita gathered up her robes and stepped into the blaze.

People averted their faces in horror. They shielded their ears against the screams of agony that would surely follow. Then suddenly, everyone shouted with joy. Sita, her body glowing like gold, stepped unscathed from the flames, while the fire god Agni shouted in pain, "O Sita, the heat of your power has burned me. Sita has burned fire!"

But yet again the rumors arose. "Perhaps that was some magic trickery she learned in Ravana's palace."

"How do we know she is not really a demon herself, with magical powers of deceit?"

And once again Rama, wavering, cried, "Go back to the forest, my wife. The people do not trust you any more. How can I?"

With Sita gone, Rama's life became miserable. Wherever he went, he saw her shining face in his mind's eye. Everywhere, he felt he heard her silver voice, and her wise words. As the years passed without Sita, the kingdom fell into decay. Misery and poverty began to scar the land.

One day, when King Rama was out hunting, he came across two boys. They were twins, bright and strong and handsome, each one a perfect reflection of the other's youth and glory. In flawless verse, they sang the story of a hero's life.

"Who is this hero of whom you sing?" asked the king.

"He is a king called Rama," they replied. "He was brave and just, once, long ago."

Rama was astonished. "Who are you?" he cried. "Who is your father?"

"No father have we," they replied, "but a mother who is the world to us. Her name is Sita."

"Take me to your mother," whispered Rama, finding in their faces his own image.

Seeing Sita once more, dignified and patient, Rama was overcome with sadness. He begged his wife's forgiveness. "I abandoned you, my queen," he said. "Come back, and rule once more with me. The kingdom is not the same without you."

Sita replied, "King, I must refuse. Take these, your sons. They are noble princes. One day they will rule in your place. My time in this life is over."

Then Sita called out to the goddess Earth, "My mother, take me back. This life is done for me. The demon Ravana is dead. My sons are no longer small children, but royal youths who have found their father. Take me back to your warm heart, my mother." And gently, quietly, without fuss, the earth opened, and swallowed her dearest daughter – Sita, strong and sweet, jewel among women. People sing about her still.

Sita's Story

Notes on

Sita's Story

The *Ramayana,* one of the best loved of Hindu stories, is generally told from Rama's point of view. The most widely known rendering of it is in Sanskrit, by the poet Valmiki. In this version, the hero's journey plays out with eloquence and drama. The battle of good against evil is recounted in great detail. Sita is more beautiful than strong, more whimsical than steady. But there are many other versions of this story, and some of them are songs sung by women. They cast Sita in a rather different light.

Valmiki's *Ramayana* includes Sita's trial by fire. Other versions simply leave it out. It is too terrible to think about. When a famous film producer made a television series based on the *Ramayana,* there was such an outcry as the episode with the fire scene approached that he had to change it, to make it seem as if Rama had never really doubted Sita. The audience was so moved by Sita's pain that they were really demanding for a sacred text to be altered, to undo an ancient injustice.

The town of Mithila, where the king Janaka found Sita, still exists in northern India. Here people feel so strongly that Sita was wronged by Rama that to this day, they say that marrying a man from Ayodhya (Rama's kingdom) will bring ill fortune to a young woman. "Ram (Rama) may have been a great man," they say, "but what did that do for our princess Sita?" My mother has said how sad she feels that Sita was so unfairly treated—as sad as if Sita were someone she knew and loved. That is how powerful this story heroine is in the imaginations of people, even today.

Sita and Rama are considered to be Lakshmi and Vishnu in human form. Rama is the seventh incarnation or form that Vishnu takes on earth, to combat evil and restore balance. In most versions, Rama and Sita feel mortal sorrows and joys, and experience the emotional struggles of humanity.

Madhu Kishwar, in an article in the women's journal Manushi, discusses the hold of Sita's story on people's imagination ("Yes to Sita, No to Ram! The Continuing Popularity of Sita in India," Manushi, 98: January-February 1997).

The Princess
Who Wished
to Be Beautiful

The princess Chitrangada rode horses as easily as other people breathe. The saddle was like a silk pillow to her. Bows and arrows were her jewelry. The music she loved best was the thunder of hooves. In her father's kingdom, the people often said, "Our king is a good man, but he is old and weak. It's the princess who really rules the kingdom!"

Out hunting one day, the princess followed the tracks of an elusive deer. She was completely intent upon the signs of the animal, its faintest of sounds. Suddenly, she reined in her horse, exclaiming, "Who's this?" There in the path of the princess lay a handsome young man, fast asleep. He wore the garments of a prince.

"Who are you, intruder, and what are you doing on my father's land?" cried the princess Chitrangada, springing lightly from her horse.

The young man flung off sleep and sat up, reaching swiftly for his sword. The princess, swifter still, placed her foot upon its flat blade and held it there, saying, "Not so fast. Who are you, bold wanderer?"

The man looked at her with contempt. "I do not answer to servants or women," he said coldly. "Release my sword, and I'll be on my way."

"Answer my question, or prepare to fight for your life," said the princess. But she stepped back from the sword.

"I am Arjuna the warrior, of royal blood," was the proud reply. "I

61

am the son of the queen Kunti, and by a divine spell, of the king of gods, Indra. I was not raised to fight with weaklings and women."

Before Chitrangada could reply, Arjuna snatched his sword from the ground, sheathed it, and walked quickly away.

"Arjuna the warrior!" cried the princess in humiliation. "For one so famous, you are rude and ill-mannered." And the princess stormed back to the palace.

Now the princess Chitrangada had never paid much attention to young men, but she could not shake the image of the warrior prince Arjuna from her mind. It annoyed her to think about him, but she could not help herself.

"Rude fellow!" she muttered. But something about the memory of him made her reach up and touch her hair, and sneak glances at herself in the palace mirrors.

Chitrangada began to hear stories about this haughty warrior prince and his brothers. "Misfortune has deprived his brothers and him of their kingdom," said the women of the court, "and they are forced to live in the forest."

"Each of the brothers is fathered by a god," went the whispers.

"The kingdom has been gambled away."

"Vishnu himself, as the cowherd god Krishna, is on their side."

And so the tales spread, until it seemed to Chitrangada that nowhere could she escape this talk of Arjuna, the arrogant warrior prince who had so humiliated her.

Chitrangada had never paid much attention to how she looked. But now, instead of using sesame oil to keep her bowstring supple, she began rubbing it on her hands and arms to soften her skin. Instead of joining the nobles on a hunt, she lingered in courtyards with the women.

The Princess Who Wished . . .

"Make me beautiful," said the princess to the ladies of the court. "I want to be beautiful."

The women, with whom the princess had rarely bothered before this, were both puzzled and amused. They combed out her hair, and braided flowers into it. They reddened her hands with henna dye. They sprinkled rose water into the folds of her clothes.

While they humored the princess, the women whispered to each other. "If truth be told," said one, "the princess Chitrangada is more brave than beautiful."

"More clever than elegant," said another.

"Who is it she's in love with?" asked a third.

"I've heard it's Arjuna!"

"She'll never set his heart on fire," they all agreed.

The princess heard the whispers, looked in her mirror, and set her chin. She went to the temple with flowers and lamps, and settled down to pray to the god of love, Manmatha. "Give me beauty, whimsical lord," she prayed, "beauty that will capture Arjuna's affections."

Laughing gently, with the exquisitely beautiful goddess Rati by his side, the god of love appeared before the princess. "As you wish, royal lady," said he. "Beauty beyond compare shall be yours."

"You shall be as lovely as I," said the goddess Rati, "but only for a year."

Lutes played and drums rolled gently, as Manmatha and Rati disappeared. Trembling, Chitrangada rushed to the temple pond, and peered in. A vision met her eyes, dark-haired, golden-skinned, slender and beautiful, perfect as the dawn.

Delirious with happiness, Chitrangada rushed to the forest in search of Arjuna. She found him in meditation, legs crossed into the lotus position, eyes closed. Startled by her presence, he opened his eyes. "Lovely lady, are you real? You must be a goddess, or a nymph of the forest," marvelled Arjuna, and he promptly forgot all about his meditation.

"Prince, my name does not matter," replied the princess.

In no time at all, the warrior prince Arjuna had fallen completely and overwhelmingly in love with this enchanting woman.

"Be my wife, share my joys and sorrows," begged Arjuna. Delighted, the princess agreed.

A year sped by as if it were a heartbeat. Chitrangada was so in love that she forgot all about her own land, her father's kingdom, and the family and friends she had unthinkingly abandoned. She was as much in love with her new and beautiful self as she was with her handsome prince. Of course, she had forgotten all about his rudeness to her— now that she was beautiful, he was gallant and loving.

Walking in the forest one day, the pair came upon an old woman. She was sobbing desperately. "Old mother, what is wrong?" asked Arjuna.

"Leave me alone," cried the woman. "Thieves have plundered the land. The little gold I had is gone. They burned my house. They took everything."

Arjuna drew his sword. "Mother, I can help you. I will find them, and restore your gold to you."

The silver-haired old woman shook her head in gloom. "It's been this way ever since our princess left," she said, wiping her eyes. "She alone can protect this kingdom. Without her we are all lost, lost!" And she began to wail and weep and tear her hair.

For the first time in close to a year, the princess began to feel a little bit foolish, and just the slightest bit guilty. She bit her lip, and her face grew hot with shame.

The Princess Who Wished . . .

"Who is this princess?" wondered Arjuna.

Soon they met a man sitting on a log with his head in his hands. "Brother, why so sad?" asked Arjuna.

"Ever since the princess Chitrangada left, the kingdom's gone to ruin," replied the man. "Bandits rule. The old king's word is weak, and his soldiers refuse to fight. We never had this sort of trouble before."

"Has this king no sons?" asked Arjuna.

"In our royal family," said the man, "there have been seven generations of single children. This king's daughter is his only child. She is the pride and strength of the kingdom. Now she is gone, and we are doomed to terrible violence and grief."

"This princess must be a remarkable woman," said Arjuna. The princess Chitrangada shuffled her feet and tried to avoid meeting his eye.

"Can you help us, noble prince?" asked the man of Arjuna. "Do you know where our princess is?"

"I know no princess like yours," replied Arjuna. "I would be glad to help, but I am on my own in this part of the forest. My brothers are scattered, and now I have this lovely lady to protect. I would not put her life in danger for anything in the world."

Chitrangada could stand it no longer. She burst out, "Brother, do not grieve. I am your princess. I am Chitrangada, and I will help you."

The man jumped up in joy. "Princess!" he exclaimed. "Is it really you? You look so different. But no matter, we have no time to lose. The robber king is advancing upon your father's palace as we speak." And he ran off shouting, "I've found our princess! We're safe. I've found the princess!"

There was no time for questions. Side by side, their horses flank to flank, Arjuna and Chitrangada raced into battle against the bandit king. Fighting together, they quickly defeated him.

Raising her banner in victory, Chitrangada noticed the old familiar calluses on her palm, where the bow rested comfortably. Her year was up. She touched her cheek, and felt the lotus bloom had gone. She looked at her ankles. They were her own strong bones again. Gone were the delicate joints, the silky hair, the sweeping eyelashes. The gifts from the god of love had vanished with the year's last moments, and she faced her husband as she really was.

"My warrior princess," said Arjuna. "I am ashamed. I remember you now. I was blinded by prejudice, and refused to admit that a woman could possibly be skilled in the arts of war. You deserved better. Will you forgive me?"

Chitrangada replied, "My anger, too, arose from shame. I was angry because you humiliated me, but I was also ashamed of myself, and wanted to be someone I was not, someone beautiful. Now I see that was foolish."

The pair returned in triumph to the old king, Chitrangada's father. He hugged them, and washed their hair with his grateful tears. "My daughter," said the old king in a voice like a quivering reed, "You are home, and light has returned to our land."

"Your beauty, princess, lies in your strength and skill," said Arjuna. "Will you come with me, and share my joys and sorrows?"

But Chitrangada replied, "I am the only heir to my father's kingdom. If I leave, who will protect our people? Forgive me. I will always treasure my year as your wife, but I cannot come with you."

Arjuna the swift, whose arrows sped so fast the wind god hid his face, who wore honor like a cloak, replied, "I understand, O princess." Joining his hands in respect, Arjuna left the strong young woman to carry out the work of her life.

Notes on

The Princess Who Wished to Be Beautiful

This story, like that of Savitri, forms part of the *Mahabharata.* Arjuna is one of the Pandava clan, sons of the king Pandu. The Pandavas, Arjuna with them, are driven into exile when the oldest of them gambles away the kingdom to their cousins and rivals, the Kaurava clan. An interesting part of the story is that the Pandava brothers share a wife, Draupadi, who is the main female character in the *Mahabharata.* Each of the brothers marries other women as well, and many romantic stories are woven about these relationships. Chitrangada's tale is one such branch story.

I heard this tale years ago from an old lady who lives in my memory as kind, strong and creative. Shenbagalakshmi was a sort of grandmother-at-large, and she told stories occasionally while also doing something else, like picking grit out of rice, or dead-heading the roses. Sometimes the stories crossed from mythology to legend to plain old gossip and back again. I remember hearing this one when I was a teenager, a time when girls often perceive intelligence or strength as burdensome, and beauty as desirable. More recently, grandmother and storyteller Lakshmi Gopalan added some details to my recollection of the story.

The Warrior Queen
of Jhansi

*In the early nineteenth cen-*tury, much of India was ruled by England. The rest was a jigsaw puzzle of rival kingdoms, among whom rumors flew as wildly as gunshots in battle. The British had arrived a century before, supposedly to trade, but had never left. The threatening shadow of their power hung over the kingdoms. If a ruler was judged to be hostile, British officials would take over his kingdom, exiling the ruler and his court, just like that.

In the exiled court of one such ruler lived a man called Moropant, and his young daughter, Manu. Manu's mother had died when she was very small. Her father loved her dearly, and could not refuse her slightest wish. So unlike most other young ladies of the time, Manu, as she grew up, did pretty much as she chose. And as they watched her playing with the children of other exiled nobles and princes, people began to sit up and take notice of her.

"She's clever," they said, when Manu beat a young prince at chess.

"And swift, and skillful," they remarked, when she coaxed her horse over the highest fences.

"She's strong," they marvelled, when Manu's swordplay was judged the best, better than that of all the young boys who learned the use of weapons in the court.

The Warrior Queen of Jhansi

"And stubborn," they added, when Manu refused to play with the princesses, and instead demanded to be taught to read and write. Learn to read and write she did. She learned the Scriptures, and strategies of war and diplomacy. She flew the highest kites in three kingdoms. She ran races. She could ride the wildest stallions in the stables. She fenced, and learned archery and the use of guns.

When Manu grew old enough to marry, the ruler of a neighboring kingdom, Jhansi, offered to take her for his wife. "A king?" mused Manu's father. "He is old, but they say he is a good man, and lonely since his wife died. And his kingdom needs an heir. Daughter, you could do worse."

So Manu was married. The year was 1842. As was the custom of that time and place, she changed her name. "I will call myself Lakshmibai, after Lakshmi, the goddess of wealth," she declared.

But the role of a royal wife was a hard one for *Rani,* or Queen, Lakshmibai. "Why must I cover my head all the time?" she chafed. "Why can't I go out riding on my own?" Once, to her royal husband's horror, she suggested that women ought to be allowed to dress like men and learn archery.

Lakshmibai startled the women of the court by announcing, "You too, ladies, should learn the arts of war and defense. Don't leave it all to men." She actually persuaded many of the women to join her, and trained a battalion of them, saying, "We are in difficult times. When war comes, we will all need to defend ourselves."

Such goings-on made the British a bit nervous. "Of course," they reasoned, "as long as the old king dies without an heir to the throne, there is no cause for worry. The Rani Lakshmibai, after all, is only a woman, and therefore can have no real power."

At the time, the governor-general, who represented the British monarch in India, was Lord Dalhousie. He had come up with a scheme to get huge tracts of Indian land under British control. "It is called," he said, "the Doctrine of Lapse. Whenever a native ruler dies without an heir, his kingdom will become part of British India."

But Lakshmibai gave birth to a boy, and the whole kingdom of Jhansi celebrated. This happiness did not last long, however, for the baby died. King, queen, and subjects alike mourned. The British watched, and waited.

The grief, and his years, wore heavily upon the king, and soon after this he lay on his deathbed. He called Lakshmibai to his side. "My brave young wife," said he, "let us adopt a child, so the kingdom will have an heir, and will not lapse to the *angrez*, the white ones. Promise me that you will rule for him until he is old enough to rule on his own."

Rani Lakshmibai sent for the child of a relative, who agreed to the king's wishes. She invited the British to send representatives to the king's bedside, so they might witness the adoption. The king read the deed that confirmed his last royal act. Then he slipped quietly into death, leaving his young queen with the most difficult job of her life.

The British refused to accept the adoption. Lord Dalhousie said, "An adopted child cannot inherit the throne. The kingdom of Jhansi has no heir. Therefore it lapses, and is part of British territory."

Lakshmibai shot back, "In the tradition of my people, an adopted child is no less a child than one born to his parents." But Dalhousie would not give in.

"We have governed the kingdom as well as you could," Lakshmibai argued. "Our subjects are happy. We built roads and bridges, and resting places for travelers. Why take our kingdom away?"

Lord Dalhousie refused the appeal. The queen tried again,

protesting, "During my husband's illness, and since his death, I have proved myself capable of controlling a large kingdom like this. You have ignored my ability to rule. Where is the justice for which you English say you are famous?"

"Jhansi will lapse," said Dalhousie, unmoving. And it did. The British placed troops in the kingdom, and the Rani was allowed to live there, but only with a small group of followers. That, they thought, was that.

But discontent with foreign rule was spreading throughout the land. The British Indian army had British officers, but Indian soldiers. From one town and village to another, from barracks to military barracks, runners brought stacks of *chapatis*, unleavened bread, with secret messages of rebellion hidden inside them. Soldiers plotted revolt against their commanding officers. Revolution brewed right under the noses of the British.

The final straw came when a new bullet cartridge was distributed by British officers to their soldiers. Its casing, greased with pork and beef fat, had to be bitten off before the bullets could be used. But Hindus consider the cow sacred, so Hindu soldiers would not use the new cartridges. Neither would Muslim soldiers, because Muslims will not eat pork, deeming it unclean. The cartridges were like salt sprinkled on old wounds of oppression. Like a powder keg igniting suddenly, Indian soldiers revolted, violently attacking their British officers all over the land, in many of the states the British had annexed. One of these states was Jhansi.

"Treason!" cried the British. They cracked down on the soldiers, calling them mutineers. Suspected ringleaders were summarily executed. Many others were thrown into prison and held there without trial.

The Warrior Queen of Jhansi

Accused of helping the rebellion, Rani Lakshmibai prepared for war. In the chaos of the soldiers' revolt, she took control of her kingdom again, and mustered her forces. "They will not defeat us," she swore. "We should not begin the battle, but we will be ready when they attack us."

The British attack was swift. Lakshmibai herself rode out at the head of her troops, urging them to fight bravely for their homeland. She guided her horse through battle with the unerring skill she had shown in her youth. Her sword flashed as swiftly as it had in the old days, when she had beaten all the young princes.

The British forces were taken aback, and withdrew. But only for a while. They returned with reinforcements. Still Rani Lakshmibai would not surrender. She enlisted the help of allies from a neighboring state, and together the armies fought Dalhousie's forces. Then a charge of British camel troops put an end to the queen's resistance.

Shattered, Lakshmibai's army retreated. She sought help from another neighboring prince. But he was a weak ally, interested only in gaining power for himself. While Lakshmibai bargained with him for his help, the British attacked again.

"I am ready," said Rani Lakshmibai, "to do my duty." She mounted her horse and rode out, her sword held high, her spirit unflagging. She died, they say, on the battlefield, with words of pride on her lips, a remarkable woman. Her story lives on still.

SHOWER OF GOLD

Notes on
The Warrior Queen of Jhansi

Rani Lakshmibai of Jhansi was by all accounts an educated young woman, accomplished in the martial arts. British records indicate that she was a skilled horsewoman, and a fine judge of horses. When she began her rule in 1853, much of India was under the control of the East India Company of England. The East India Company originally purported to be a trading outfit. By the eighteenth century, however, the British Crown had an official representative in India, the governor-general. In Lakshmibai's time, this was Lord Dalhousie. After the revolt by Indian soldiers, which British historians called "the Mutiny of 1857," and Indian historians have sometimes called "the first War of Independence," the British queen Victoria was proclaimed Empress of India, and all such rebellions were firmly squelched. Some people think the British, who held strong views on the proper place and behavior of women, had a difficult time accepting that a woman could be as forceful and as brave as Lakshmibai was. Queen Victoria, they point out, never rode into battle at the head of her troops!

Lakshmibai's story, in history and legend, is celebrated in Joyce Lebra-Chapman's book, *The Rani of Jhansi: A Study in Female Heroism in India* (Honolulu: University of Hawaii Press, 1986).

Vishnu's Bride

Long ago a hunter chieftain built a temple in the jungle, a temple to the god Vishnu. Around it, in later years, there grew a town, with bustling markets and traders coming and going. The heart of the town was always the temple. It stood right in the center, and the four main streets of the town led to the temple's four great wooden doors.

Now in that temple was employed a priest, and his name was Vishnuchitta. One of his tasks was to clear the weeds around the stands of *tulasi,* or holy basil, that grew in the temple garden. One early morning, as usual, he began this daily chore. Suddenly, he gave a startled cry. A baby girl lay on the hard ground, smiling and dimpled, looking as content as if she were in a rocking cradle.

"Like Lakshmi, you bring light into this garden," marvelled Vishnuchitta. He picked up the child, saying, "I will raise you as my own, and I will call you Kodai, which means 'she who was born of the earth.' Like Sita, you are the earth's child."

Kodai grew up a laughing child, strong and sweet-tempered. From an early age, she began to help her adoptive father with his temple duties. He gave her the special job of stringing garlands of flowers which he offered in the temple as part of the daily prayer. Always about the girl there hung the delicate scent of *tulasi.*

As Kodai grew older, people began saying to her father, "You must

75

find a young man to be a good husband to your lovely daughter." But Kodai startled them all by her reply. "Bring me no young men to look upon. I will marry no one but Vishnu himself."

Now the priest had always been a most devout follower of Vishnu, but as his strange and beautiful daughter grew older, he began noticing odd things happening. Poems came into his mind that had never been there before. He found himself able to understand the scriptures in greater detail and with sharper clarity than he had ever known. Somehow, he knew that all this had to do with the child who had come from the *tulasi* bed.

Kodai, spurning human men, began to compose songs and poems of her own. She sang love songs to Vishnu, about the time when he came to earth as Krishna the handsome, dark-skinned cowherd. She sang of how he stole butter from the kitchens when he was an infant, and the hearts of the milkmaids when he grew to be a young man. And she sang of herself, Krishna's beloved, and asked only to be by his side.

"The image of my dreams," said Kodai, "is in the temple of the next town of Srirangam." Sometimes, while she made the flower garlands ready for the temple, she playfully draped them about her own neck, and imagined herself the dark god's bride.

One day, Vishnuchitta was getting ready for the evening prayers at the temple, when he noticed a long, black hair snagged in one of the garlands. Sternly, he said to Kodai, "Daughter, you know it is forbidden to wear these holy flowers before they are offered in worship. Mere mortals must not wear them for their own pleasure, or even inhale their scent."

Kodai stood silent, a look of panic on her face at having been discovered. Angrily, Vishnuchitta left the room.

Vishnu's Bride

In the evening, the priest performed the prayer ceremony without using any flower garlands. That night, as Vishnuchitta settled into sleep, the god Vishnu entered his mind in a dream, saying, "Where are those flowers, graced by the lady Kodai? Those flowers worn by her have a special fragrance, O Vishnuchitta."

"Lord, forgive me," begged Vishnuchitta. "I could not use those flowers in worship. My daughter was vain, and wore them without thinking."

"Oh no," said Vishnu to the priest. "She wore them with love, and with love I will accept them. In centuries to come your daughter will be known as Andal, or 'she who rules the Lord.' "

And Vishnuchitta was jolted awake. "This is indeed a divine child," he said to himself.

Kodai remained adamant in refusing marriage with anyone but Vishnu. "He whom I love lives in the temple in Srirangam," said she.

Finally, heavy-hearted, her father agreed. A marriage procession escorted Kodai to the temple in Srirangam. Drummers flexed their nimble fingers, and pipers played triumphant wedding music. Kodai, lovely and determined, dressed in bridal silks and jewels, stepped over the threshold. She walked past the worshippers, through a second doorway, and up to the innermost sanctum of the temple that housed the great stone image of her beloved. Past the point where all but the priest must stop, past the great flickering flames of giant oil lamps, right up to the sacred sculpture. She touched the blessed stone. Without a backward glance at her fond old father, she climbed up onto the coils of the great serpent Adisesha, who is Vishnu's couch.

And then she disappeared.

SHOWER OF GOLD

Notes on
Vishnu's Bride

Lakshmi, the goddess at Vishnu's side, is sometimes shown in two forms—Sridevi, the goddess of wealth; and Bhoodevi, the earth goddess. Andal, the legends say, was actually Bhoodevi, who came to our world to follow a path of love, and was found by Vishnuchitta under the basil plant.

Andal, or Kodai, really did live in about the eighth century A.D. in what is today the Indian state of Tamilnadu. Her songs are part of a tradition that remains unbroken to this day. Every year, from mid-December to mid-January, a poem of thirty verses composed by Andal is sung in towns and villages in southern India. Recorded versions are available on tape and CD, and the regional radio network plays one song for each of the sacred days. I remember, as a child, flipping through a Tamil picture book that my parents kept in our little house-hold shrine. It was an edition of Andal's famous poem. Each page had a bright picture of Krishna the cowherd god—playing tricks on his family, overpowering a rogue elephant, stealing the clothes of milkmaids while they bathed in the river.

Recently, I learned that a strange prayer ritual still takes place daily in the Vishnu temple in Andal's hometown. Each night, a priest places a flower garland around the neck of a statue of Andal. In the morning the same garland, now withered, is used as an offering at Vishnu's shrine.

Vishnu's Bride

The chieftain with whom this story begins was called Villi. The town came to be known as Villiputtur, or "new town of Villi." Since Andal came to earth there, it then became known as Srivilliputtur, or Sri's (Lakshmi's) new town of Villi. All these centuries later, that is still its name.

The Love Story
of Roopmati and
Baz Bahadur

One day a young sultan named Baz Bahadur went hunting in the forest with a group of nobles from his court. "Hark, friends!" he cried to his hunting companions, "A deer! A buck, with splendid antlers. There he goes!" But the tawny brown deer with the twelve pronged antlers vanished quickly in the thick growth of trees.

Baz Bahadur dismounted from his horse. "Wait here," he told his friends, "I'll follow it on foot."

Drawn by glimpses of the deer, Baz Bahadur wandered further and further into the dense growth of trees. Suddenly, the warm summer breeze lifted a melody his way. It was sung by a voice like no other he had ever heard before.

"What nymph of the woods is this who sings such a beautiful song?" cried Baz Bahadur. He forgot all about the deer, and followed the singing voice instead.

Coming to a clearing, Baz Bahadur stopped short. A group of women, dressed in the rich clothes and tasselled jewels of Hindu nobility, were picking flowers in the forest. They were an elegant group. Baz Bahadur stood embarrassed, unsure what to do next. *For they are Hindu women, thought he, and I a Muslim king. It would not be right to intrude upon their privacy.*

But he could not take his eyes off one of them. It was she who was singing, and her voice was more beautiful than any bells crafted by human hands. Almost in a trance, Baz Bahadur stepped forward, not caring any more if the women thought him rude, or a madman. He bowed to the young woman with the golden voice, saying, "Forgive me, princess, for a princess you must be, and I am bewitched by your song."

The women in the group threw their wraps over their faces in horror at being surprised in this unseemly fashion. But the young woman with the haunting voice said calmly, "I am the princess Roopmati, daughter of the king of Mandu."

"Your voice, princess," said Baz Bahadur, "could lead me to the gates of hell, and I would go gladly."

"It is a gift," said the princess, "from the goddess Rewa, whose sacred river graces my father's kingdom of Mandu."

"Come, lady," said one of the other women. "Do not stay to speak with this barbarian."

"Your father the king would think ill of you," scolded another, "for speaking so boldly to a strange man, with your face uncovered."

"Get away, sir," warned a third. "This is no ordinary court singer. Our princess is known throughout the kingdom for the poetry and music she composes."

"Come," they urged, tugging at Roopmati's silk robes. "Come home where this wild man will not trouble you."

Baz Bahadur lost all reason. "Princess," he cried. "Your beauty, your talent, and your gentleness have snatched my heart away. Marry me, so I do not lose my mind with love for you."

"Shame!" shouted the women. "How could you? And she a Hindu princess!"

To their utter astonishment, the princess Roopmati replied, "If the

goddess Rewa sends her waters through your kingdom, I will be your wife."

"What?" shrieked the women. "Your father will have him beheaded. You will cause a war! Your father will have you beheaded! It's you who have lost your mind, Princess Roopmati."

Baz Bahadur touched his hand to his forehead in farewell, and left, saying, "The goddess will come. I am sure of it."

"Don't listen to him," said Roopmati's companions. "He's a savage Muslim. He doesn't even believe in the goddess. She will surely heap bad luck upon him." But Roopmati smiled, and in her heart she spoke to the goddess.

Back in his palace, Baz Bahadur could not shake from his mind the image of the beautiful princess with the voice like a flute.

"Royal prince," said his ministers. "The courts are waiting for your judgment." Baz Bahadur waved them away.

"Your Highness," pleaded his servants. "The cooks have prepared your favorite dishes, the musicians their finest works. Noble guests are awaiting your presence." Baz Bahadur ignored them all.

Finally, with stealth and secrecy, came word of Roopmati. From trusted servant, through bribed horseman, to a loyal friend of Baz Bahadur's, the news arrived.

"Her parents have found out about your meeting in the woods," said Baz Bahadur's faithful friend to him. "Her father threatened to kill her, rather than let her marry a Muslim."

"What did she say to that?" whispered Baz Bahadur.

"She told her parents she would die rather than marry anyone else."

"Where is she?" demanded Baz Bahadur. "I must go to her."

SHOWER OF GOLD

"She sends you this letter." And the friend handed Baz Bahadur a note.

Reading the letter from his love, Baz Bahadur grew pale. "Roopmati's mother has prevailed upon her father the king to set aside his sword," he cried, "but my love is now locked up in a room in the palace. She spends her time weeping and praying, and singing songs of sorrow. I must go to her."

"There is more," said the friend. "Roopmati awoke from her sleep yesterday to see the goddess Rewa standing before her."

"Yes?" Baz Bahadur was impatient.

"The goddess told her that she will soon be free, and united with you, my friend. And that very soon, in your kingdom, there will spring forth a new source of water from the River Rewa."

Baz Bahadur jumped up in joy. "The goddess has spoken," he proclaimed. "It is the sign she was waiting for, my princess Roopmati."

That very night, Baz Bahadur and his army attacked Roopmati's father's kingdom of Mandu. Taken by surprise, the armies of Mandu surrendered. Baz Bahadur entered the palace, and raced up the steps to the tower room where Roopmati was waiting.

At the very moment that Roopmati was reunited with her lover, something strange and wonderful happened. A fount of clear, cold water from the River Rewa burst forth in Baz Bahadur's kingdom. The goddess had kept her promise.

Baz Bahadur and Roopmati ruled together as king and queen, sharing joy and sorrow, war and peace. Together, they are buried in a tomb in the northern Indian town of Sarangpur. Their love, people say, will never die. In the building housing the tomb of these lovers, there is said to live a strange echo. If you call out, "Roopmati," the echo answers, "Baz Bahadur!"

Roopmati and Baz Bahadur

Notes on
The Love Story of Roopmati and Baz Bahadur

This is the Romeo and Juliet story of fifteenth century India – an account of star-crossed lovers who stayed true to one another. Set against Muslim and Hindu communities divided by barriers of suspicion, the pair ruled together for only a brief time, and their lives ended tragically. Baz Bahadur was killed in battle by a rival ruler, who took Roopmati captive and tried to force her to join his harem. Rather than give in, it is said, she sang one last song of love for Baz Bahadur. Then, drinking a cup of poison, she took her own life. Although Roopmati's songs and poems were never written down, some of them have survived in the folk lyrics of the Indian desert state of Rajasthan.

I first came across the story of Roopmati when I was about fourteen, in a Hindi language class in Delhi. Completing homework assignments on it failed to rob the tale of its power, and it has stayed with me all these years. I found it again in a retelling by Shanti Mahajan on the Internet, at http://www.shishubharati.org. When I talked to Shanti later about the story, she told me, "Roopmati seemed like me. She played music. She had dreams. And I thought it was sad and unfair that in so many stories girls and women are told what to do."

Roopmati's tale is mentioned in *Great Women of India*, Swami Madhavananda and Ramesh Chandra Majumdar, editors (Calcutta: Advaita Ashrama Publications, 1993).

The Eight Sons of Ganga

The king Shantanu loved to walk on the banks of the sacred river Ganga, listening to the birds and watching the water as it tumbled and danced on its way. One day, he saw a woman emerging from the water, shedding silver droplets from her long black hair.

Struck by the woman's beauty, Shantanu exclaimed, "Who are you, lady? You must be some spirit of the water."

The woman laughed in reply, and the king quite lost his heart. "Lovely lady," he begged, "marry me and be my queen."

But the woman smiled, and answered, "Find another queen, O king, for there are things about me that you cannot understand."

The king insisted, saying, "I will do anything for you."

"Very well," said the mysterious woman. "I will marry you, but listen well. Here are the conditions I lay down. First, do not question anything I do—not anything. Second, ask not who I am or where I came from."

The king promised. "I don't need to know who you are or where you came from, and I would not dream of questioning your slightest wish."

"Break this promise," she warned, "and I will leave you."

A week rolled by, then a month, then a year. "I am the happiest king on earth," declared Shantanu.

The Eight Sons of Ganga

In time the queen bore a baby boy, with chubby limbs and smiling face. The king was ecstatic. "Roll the drums!" he cried. "Sound the trumpets! A prince has been born."

But the queen, without a word, took the infant down to the river, and cast him into the rolling waters. The king was about to cry out at this cruel act. Then he remembered his promise, and held his tongue.

Another year passed. Another baby boy was born. Again, the queen calmly took the infant and threw him into the river Ganga. Shantanu bit his lip and shed a tear, but kept silent.

The queen bore seven sons in all. Each one she threw into the river, and watched, smiling, as the waters closed over his head. Each time, the king's heart felt crushed with anger and sorrow.

Finally, the time came for the queen to give birth to the king's eighth child. Once again, a prince was born. Once again, the queen reached for the infant. This time the king could stand it no longer. He burst out, "How can you be so cruel? You've killed seven innocent babies, and you're getting ready to murder an eighth! What demon world do you come from, heartless woman?"

The queen sighed. "King, listen well," she said. "I am Ganga, goddess of the sacred river that bears my name. I must leave you, for you have broken your promise. But before I go, I will tell you a story.

"Years ago, eight *devas* chanced by the hermitage of the *rishi* Vashishtha, and spied his darling cow Nandini and her dark-eyed calf. They stole the cow and calf, and took them back to *devaloka,* the home of the gods. But Vashishtha discovered their crime, and he cursed them to be born again as people, into the world of human cares and woes from which all souls seek release.

"The *devas* begged for mercy, so Vashishtha said to them, 'If the goddess Ganga agrees to help you, she can shorten your journey in the mortal world, and send your souls back to the realms of the gods.'"

"Those *devas* were your babies!" cried the thunderstruck king Shantanu.

"Those *devas* were my babies," replied Ganga.

"And the eighth?"

"This eighth was the *deva* whose hands led the cow away. Since he is more to blame, he must live longer in his human form. Fear not, O king, I will not hurl him into the river. Here is your son, Bhishma. He will live to be old, and kings will honor him. In a great battle that will overtake the world, he will be on the side of justice, and they will call him Grandfather."

Ganga handed her last-born son to the king. She smiled farewell. Tossing her long dark hair, she walked down the steep stone steps, right into the river. Where the waters closed over her head, there were only translucent green weeds, and the sudden splash of a leaping fish or two.

Notes on
The Eight Sons of Ganga

Like the stories of Savitri and Chitrangada, this is one of the branch tales of the *Mahabharata*. It forms part of the everyday story lore of many Hindu homes. Rivers hold great power and meaning in Hindu tradition, and all rivers are held to represent the mighty Ganga. In many Hindu homes, you will find small sealed copper pots, usually placed in the household shrine, containing water from the river

The Eight Sons of Ganga

Ganga. The goddess Ganga is known for her loving mercy. It is believed that even the worst of humans are made pure again when they bathe in her forgiving waters.

Today, overcrowding and poor waste management have polluted the river Ganga, or Ganges. Much of the water from her upper reaches has been diverted into canals. Sewage, industrial waste, and farm pesticide runoff have fouled the river. There is now a Ganga Action Plan in effect, to clean the waters of this mighty river, and restore her beauty, of which the ancient stories speak.

Bhishma the Grandfather, son of Ganga, plays an important role in the *Mahabharata.* He is the much beloved mentor of the Pandava brothers, and his reflections on the agonies of warfare and the bitterness of victory make for some of the epic's most stirring passages.

I first found this story when I was about twelve years old, in C. Rajagopalachari's classic retelling of the *Mahabharata* (Bombay: Bharatiya Vidya Bhavan, 9ed., 1968). I have since heard a number of oral versions of it.

She Who
Showers Gold

Over a thousand years ago, in the southern part of the land we now call India, there lived a holy man named Shankara. He had only very few possessions—a rough cloth to cover his body, a pair of wooden sandals, and a wooden bowl. But his mind was filled with prayer, and his heart was rich with love. That brought him happiness greater than the gold of many kingdoms.

Once, Shankara was on a pilgrimage, criss-crossing the land from south to north and west to east. He walked across sandy beaches, over high, cold mountains, from glacier lakes to steamy river deltas. Wherever he went he spoke to people of how all that is divine is really one, only taking different forms. Wherever he went, crowds gathered to hear him talk, and wondered at his simple words and clear ideas.

Once, after a long day on the dusty road, Shankara entered a village. Now it was the custom of that time to treat pilgrims as honored guests. They could ask for food, and no one would refuse them. So bowl in hand, Shankara walked down the main street. In front of a tiny house, its walls plastered roughly with mud, he saw a woman. At his approach, the woman cried out, "Oh, I am unfortunate, unfortunate!" She wept, and would not stop.

"Mother, what distresses you?" asked Shankara.

"Holiness," replied the woman, "I heard you were coming, and I

90

ran and searched my poor house for a fitting meal to offer you. But we have nothing to eat ourselves, and so all I have to give you is this." The woman opened her hand. In it was one small gooseberry. It was a sour, poor fruit, hardly fit to be eaten, let alone offered to a guest.

"It's all I have," repeated the woman, wiping her tears.

"Do not worry about me. What of yourself, good lady, and your family?" asked Shankara, concerned. "Have you nothing else with which to feed yourselves?"

Embarrassed, the woman whispered, "No, holy one, nothing."

"Have you children? What of them?"

"Only one, a daughter," said the woman unhappily, "and that is worst of all. She is to be married soon. Only the goddess must provide for her wedding, for I, her mother, cannot."

Shankara's heart was filled with compassion for the woman. Into his mind came words of beauty, words that he sang to the goddess Lakshmi. And from his lips there came a chant. Its rhythms were strong and bright, like the goddess herself, who sits on a lotus flower, guarded by two white elephants; who holds the keys to wealth and worldly happiness; whose mercy and kindness know no bounds.

From Shankara's lips came words of praise for Lakshmi, "She Who Showers Gold," who has everything, yet gives it all away, over and over, to those in need. Verse after verse he sang, seeming to forget everything around him—the dusty street, the rough mud hut, the woman and her grief.

The poor woman stood listening, clutching the berry in her hand. Then suddenly she cried out in amazement. She opened her hand, and stared in disbelief. Lying in her palm was something hard and cool and shiny. The sour little berry had turned into a splendid gold coin.

"Why, this is a miracle," gasped the woman. "This can surely feed the guests at my daughter's wedding."

Then the woman nearly fainted. Because all around her fell a shower of gold coins, thousands of them, enough to pay for a hundred weddings. She fell down in awe and wonder, saying, "Thank you, holy one, but this is enough! One coin will suffice for me. What will I do with all this wealth?"

Shankara said, "This is not my doing, lady. It is the goddess Lakshmi, generous and giving, who has granted you this gift."

But the woman persisted. "But what will I do with it all? I have never even seen so much money before."

Shankara replied, "Mother, use it wisely, and well. Would you question what Lakshmi herself has chosen to give you?" And the woman promised, gratefully, to use her new wealth wisely, and to use it well.

The woman kept her promise. Of all the riches that were showered upon her, she kept only what she needed. She made sure the poor of a hundred villages ate richly at her daughter's wedding. And every day, at dusk, she lighted an oil lamp to guide Lakshmi to her house, and recited the hymn that Shankara had sung to the goddess —the hymn that had freed her family from the burden of poverty.

She Who Showers Gold

Notes on
She Who Showers Gold

Shankara, sometimes called Adi Shankara (meaning the first, or original, Shankara) lived in India, in about the eighth century A.D. He led a movement to reform Hinduism, and make Hindu teachings meaningful to the lives of ordinary people. The places of worship and study he established in his travels are still important religious centers. This legend is about a hymn to the goddess Lakshmi ("She Who Showers Gold") that Shankara is really said to have composed. This particular chant emphasizes the importance of Lakshmi in the Hindu tradition. Worldly wealth, in moderation, is seen as a necessary part of life. Its opposite, involuntary poverty, is negative and undesirable. In contrast, giving up worldly wealth voluntarily is seen as a good or noble act—one that carries great spiritual merit in this and future lives.

Some years ago, my mother gave me a little "book" of this hymn, printed in the Tamil language on parchment of a goldenrod color, and bound accordion-style with silk thread. "Keep it," she said. "It's good to have in the house." And she told me the story of how Shankara is said to have composed the hymn.

The Magic Tree

Many years ago there lived a young woman who was not very happy. This was because her husband, although he was kind and loving, was never home. He was by trade a tinker, a mender of pots and pans. He was often on the road, earning meager wages for very hard work. Another cause of the young woman's sorrow was her husband's mother, who lived with them. All day long the mean old woman nagged her daughter-in-law.

"Cook this!" the mother-in-law would demand. "Clean that! Sweep the floor! Fetch water from the well!" Hard and long the poor young woman slaved, until she grew quite worn and tired.

One day, when the mother-in-law was out, the young woman bent over an iron pot. She stirred the lentils and vegetables in there, and watched them bubble and boil for dinner. Suddenly there was a knock on the door.

"Perhaps it is my husband, come back a few days early," said the woman to herself, opening the door.

An old beggar man stood there, bowl in hand. "Gentle lady, I am hungry," he said. "Have you some scraps to spare for an old man?"

The young woman took pity on the beggar. "Come in, grandfather," she said, and invited him into the kitchen. She spooned rice

94

into the old man's bowl and topped it with a generous helping of the lentils and vegetables.

The old man ate as if he had not seen such food in a lifetime. He was so hungry that when he was done, only tiny portions of rice and lentils were left. Then the old man took his leave, crying, "Blessings upon you, kind lady, and upon your husband, and the children you will have. Blessings upon their children, and their children's children, for a hundred generations!"

Now of course, when the mother-in-law came home, she was furious. "All that rice!" she cried. "You just poured it all into some wretched beggar's bowl. Now all the lazy and jobless will beat a path to this door." And the mother-in-law began throwing pots and pans about in her rage. "Get out of this house. I never want to see your face again!"

The woman, afraid, ran out the door as fast as she could. She ran and ran until she was all out of breath. Then she collapsed under a tree. Only then did she realize she had run clear out of town and was in a thick forest. Hearing muffled voices approaching, she quickly climbed into the tree. She pulled its thick leaves and stout branches across her body to hide herself. Then she sat there very quietly, listening and watching.

Two demon women, *rakshasis,* lived in that tree. Their voices came closer, as they returned home. With grunts and thumps, they climbed into the tree. To the woman's alarm, the entire tree soon lifted off the ground, and began flying through the air. The woman held on with all her strength.

"To the Land with the Sands of Gold, shall we, little sister?" screeched one of the *rakshasis.*

"Of course sister, big sister, whatever you wish," crowed the other.

While the woman watched wide-eyed, the *rakshasis* flew the tree across the ocean, to an island beach where the sand shone and sparkled. Parking the tree, the *rakshasi* sisters wandered off into the ocean for a swim. Cautiously, the young woman got down from the magic tree, and gingerly stepped on the sand. Every grain underfoot was pure, dazzling gold.

Quickly the woman tore a strip from the end of her sari. Swiftly, she tied up the ends, and filled this cloth bag with as much gold sand as it would hold. Then she climbed back into the tree and waited.

When the *rakshasis* returned, they flew the tree back home to its native forest. Soon, they were asleep, just a whisper away from where the young woman sat. Waiting until their snores shook the ground, the woman crept quietly down. She ran, heart thumping, all the way home.

Joyfully, the young woman showed her mother-in-law the bag of gold sand. But instead of being grateful, the mother-in-law snapped at her, "Is that all you could think to bring back? A whole beach of gold and you've brought us a thimbleful."

Now the mother-in-law really wanted to see this beach of gold for herself. So the next night she said to her daughter-in-law, "Take me to this forest. Show me this tree."

The young woman protested, but the mother-in-law persisted. So, giving in, the young woman took her mother-in-law to the forest and pointed out the tree to her.

"Give me a hand up," commanded the mother-in-law. She was rather plump, possibly from eating too much and doing little work. With much effort, she managed to climb into the tree. Then she waved her daughter-in-law away, "Go home. You're not coming this time. I'll do this alone, thank you very much. Go on, now, shoo!" Shaking her head, the young woman went home.

Meanwhile, up in the tree, the mother-in-law rubbed her hands in glee. She chuckled with delight as she imagined the riches she was

about to collect. "Rich!" she said out loud. "I'll be rich!"

At dusk, the *rakshasis* came lumbering to the tree, and climbed into its knotty branches. The mother-in-law could just about reach out and touch them. "Travel time," cackled the *rakshasis*, as the tree lifted off and headed for the ocean. Soon it was flying over the water, so low that the mother-in-law could almost feel the salt spray.

"Big sister, where to?" screamed one of the *rakshasis*.

"Little sister, I have a terrible hunger for some fish tonight," grumbled the other. "Fly us to the Land of the Flying Fish. There I will lie on the beach with my mouth open, and let the fish fly in. Go, little sister, go!"

"No, no!" cried the mother-in-law from the branch above, unable to stop herself. "The Land with the Sands of Gold, that's where I'm headed!"

"What!" shrieked the *rakshasis*. "Who are you, and what are you doing in our tree?" And forthwith they stopped in mid-flight, turned the tree upside down, and dumped the mother-in-law out—right into the ocean. Nowadays, some say she is that rock over there, sticking up out of the water, searching for the way to the beach with the gold sands. Some say she is swimming her hardest, but has a long way to go still.

As for the young woman, when her husband got back they looked for the mother-in-law, although, to be quite honest, they did not look too hard. The woman shared the small sack of gold sand with her husband. They agreed it was enough to keep them in comfort the rest of their lives. "Let's not be greedy," they promised each other. "We don't need any more."

The young woman never went near that forest again. She never, never told another soul about the magic tree or the Land with the Sands of Gold.

The Magic Tree

Notes on
The Magic Tree

Although this story has the rhythm and texture of an oral tale, it is sometimes said to be related to an ancient written story collection called the *Panchatantra*—literally, "five frames." The original was written in Sanskrit, perhaps as early as 200 BC, possibly by a scholar named Vishnu Sharma. It is now long lost. However, it has survived in a number of translations, first into Arabic, and later into English. This particular story is thought by some to be a later addition to the original text.

The *Panchatantra* is a set of stories-within-stories, much like nesting boxes. The main frame is of an anxious king hiring a teacher for his three sons, who are completely uninterested in their lessons. The teacher uses stories to drum sense into the heads of the princes. Stories from the *Panchatantra* are still very popular in India. They were at one time serialized into a Sunday comic strip in a major newspaper. They are still published in comic book format, and occasionally aired in radio programs for children. There is a wide range of female characters in the *Panchatantra* tales, not all of them portrayed in a favorable light.

Like "The Daughter-in-Law Who Got Her Way," this particular tale is about a family relationship between women. Here goodness and hard work win over greed. I encountered this story many years ago, when I was in elementary school, and my class dramatized it. I have to confess to playing the role of the tree!

My Name
Is Illusion

A baby was about to be born to the nobleman Vasudeva and his wife Devaki. The waiting couple were filled with fear. It was said that this baby would grow up to kill the tyrannical king Kamsa, and liberate the people. Devaki and Vasudeva were sure that if Kamsa heard this prediction, he would find some way to harm the child.

Just as they feared, Kamsa heard the rumors and set a guard about the house of Devaki and Vasudeva. He was determined to end the child's life as soon as it began.

It was in fact the blue-skinned god Vishnu, the god of order and balance, who was to be born to Devaki as the infant Krishna. And Vishnu saw that Kamsa had evil in his heart. So he called out to the goddess who can take many forms, "Great goddess, come in the form of deepest sleep. Help the world of people in its time of need."

The goddess arrived, and the universe lighted up when she smiled. "It's not for nothing they sometimes call me Mahamaya, 'Great Illusion,'" she said. "What do you wish me to do?"

And Vishnu said to her, "The wicked king Kamsa seeks to destroy the child who is fated to kill him. Help us. Cast your spell upon Kamsa, and upon all his armies. Swordsmen and horsemen, shield-bearers and trumpeters—spare no one. Make sure they grow drowsy and fall into the deepest sleep. Then you too must be born on earth, in a humble home, to parents without wealth or power."

The goddess agreed. And Vishnu, before arriving on earth, appeared in the dreams of two men. They were the nobleman Vasudeva and a cowherd named Nanda. Vishnu told them of the plan, promising, "Exchange infants at birth, and all will be well."

So it came to pass that at the deepest hour of night, Vishnu was born to Devaki as the infant Krishna. He was smiling and chubby, and so dark that there were hints of blue in the color of his skin. At the same time there was rejoicing in the humble home of the cowherd Nanda and his wife Yashoda, at the birth of a beautiful baby girl. Her eyes and hair were as dark as midnight.

Swiftly Vasudeva raced across town, a swaddled bundle in his arms, stumbling over the sleeping Kamsa and his armies, to the hut of the cowherd Nanda. When he returned, he held the sleeping baby girl.

When Kamsa awoke he suspected trickery. He felt his heavy head, exclaiming, "We have been drugged! Never have I slept like this." All around him, his soldiers were waking up, shaking their heads and rubbing the sleep from their eyes.

Furious, Kamsa rushed into the street, nearly knocking down a toothless old woman who was selling bananas.

"Krishna has been born," cried the old woman joyfully, recovering her balance and clutching at the big hands of bananas she held.

"Old fool!" swore Kamsa.

"Now we'll be free!" exclaimed the woman, not realizing she was talking to the tyrant himself.

Kamsa would ordinarily have ordered her executed on the spot but now he merely brushed her aside. He rushed to the house of the nobleman Vasudeva, and ran past the guards, right into the inner rooms. There Devaki lay resting, holding in her arms a radiant infant.

Kamsa snatched the baby from Devaki's arms. He was about to dash its head against the stone steps, when all of a sudden, there was a fearful roar. The infant vanished. In her place was the goddess Mahamaya, with eight arms and a cloud of black hair.

"Kamsa, proud Kamsa," said the goddess sternly. "Your end is nearer than you think."

Kamsa shrank away in fear, his eyes fixed on the shiny sword the goddess wielded. "What—what do you mean?"

"Oh, you've nothing to fear from me," said she. "He is born, the one who will bring your days on this earth to an end. Beware of Krishna, Kamsa. He has come to earth."

Kamsa began to shiver. "Who are you?" he asked at last, putting his hands up to shelter his eyes from her bright light.

"My name," said the goddess, "is sometimes sleep, sometimes illusion. Sometimes I fog the mind, and sometimes I cloud the eye. Reflect upon your life, Kamsa. Not much of it is left." And whipping her sword through the air, inches from Kamsa's raised hand, the goddess vanished.

Far, far away, she reappeared, in the rocky vastness of the Vindhya Mountains. And just as she had predicted, Vishnu in the form of the infant Krishna, blue-skinned and playful, grew to be a mighty warrior, and sent the evil Kamsa to his next life.

The goddess, it is said, still lives in those Vindhya Mountains. From there, she can look out over south and north, within hailing distance of people and gods. She keeps watch, just in case she is ever needed again.

My Name Is Illusion

Notes on
My Name Is Illusion

Separating the northern plains from the great plateau of the Indian subcontinent are the mountains called the Vindhyas. The story goes that once the Vindhyas tried to compete with the tallest mountains on earth, the Himalayas. The Vindhyas grew in arrogance and self-importance—and height. Finally, the *rishi* Agastya asked them to stop growing until he journeyed south and returned. The mountains agreed. The *rishi* went south, and never came back. The Vindhyas, only four thousand feet high, are still waiting.

This story of Krishna's birth stars the goddess who lives in those mountains. It is an example of sacred geography, in which real places have mythological characters and events associated with them. Some say Mahamaya is an example of a goddess who is more ancient than Hinduism, but has been assimilated into Hindu lore. Details about the goddess in the form of Vindhyavasini, "she who lives in the Vindhyas," can be found in the book, *Devi: Goddesses of India* edited by John Stratton Hawley and Donna Marie Wulff (Berkeley: University of California Press, 1996).

In Hindu stories, Krishna, who grew up to destroy Kamsa, was also charioteer and guide to the warrior Arjuna, in the great war that forms the heart of the *Mahabharata*. The part of the Hindu scriptures known as the *Bhagavad Gita* is said to have been told to Arjuna by Krishna at the beginning of this war.

As a child I heard many times the stories that overlap in this tale of Krishna's birth.

Kali's Curse

In a village called Tenali in the south of India, there lived a boy named Rama, whose parents worried about him. They worried because he laughed so much. True, he made other people laugh as well, but "What use is that," they wondered, "when the world's a serious place? It certainly won't help him earn a living."

But Tenali Rama only laughed and replied, "If the world's a serious place, that is the world's problem, not mine."

A wise old man passing by heard the parents lamenting. He said to young Rama, "Perhaps I can help. I will teach you a special chant. Learn it well. Then go to the temple of the goddess Kali. Recite a thousand times these sacred words, and Kali herself will help you find your path in life."

So Rama and his parents agreed. The old man taught Tenali Rama the secret words, just as he had promised. "A thousand times, now, don't forget," he cautioned.

"I won't, grandfather," promised Rama.

Rama's parents consulted an astrologer, who studied his star charts and helped them pick a good day for this great event to occur. Rama bathed, and dressed in clean clothes. Then, as he had been told to do, he went to the Kali temple.

Rama walked through the first courtyard of the temple, then

through the second, until he was finally in the innermost part of the building where the image of Kali stood. Even carved in stone, she was most wondrously fierce. Rama gave her a quick respectful greeting. Then he settled down to his task.

For the next hour, not a single smile did Tenali Rama crack. He just chanted, and chanted, and chanted. Five hundred times he recited the special verses he had been taught. Seven hundred. Nine hundred. A thousand. And as the thousandth repetition left his lips, with a flash of bright light and a clap of thunder, there in front of him stood Kali herself. In fierceness, her image was not a patch on her. She had a thousand heads. From each one of her mouths hung a long red tongue. A thousand heads, each gar-landed with a necklace of skulls. A thousand heads she had—but only two hands.

Upon seeing her, instead of being terrified, Tenali Rama began to laugh. He laughed so hard and so loud that he clutched his stomach and rolled on the ground. The little mice that lived in the temple off the offerings of devotees came scurrying round to investigate the strange sounds.

"And what is so funny?" demanded the goddess. She was not used to this response. Most people died of fright when they saw her, some-times quite literally. "First you use my special chant to call me, then you split your sides laughing. Speak up, fool!"

"O goddess," gasped Rama, when finally he gained control of himself. "You know that heads have noses. And noses sometimes catch colds. Now we humans have an awful time trying to blow our noses when that happens—and we only have one nose to worry about handling with our two hands! When I saw you I wondered how you, who also have only two hands, can possibly manage to cope with a thousand runny noses!" The thought threw Tenali Rama into convulsions of laughter all over again.

The goddess was not amused. She said frostily, "Since you are such a joker at such a young age, you must spend the rest of your life making a living from laughter. You shall be a *vikatakavi,* a jester." She meant it to punish, since jesters hardly make what one might call a living.

Rama considered. Then he remarked with interest, *"Vi-ka-ta-ka-vi.* A jester. What a fascinating word. It's a palindrome. It reads the same from right to left as from left to right—*vi-ka-ta-ka-vi.*" And written in the Sanskrit language, विकटकवि, it does indeed.

Now the goddess was impressed. Not only had this young man dared to laugh at her, but he had found something humorous and interesting even in a curse. So she relented, adding, "Yes, you'll be a jester, but you'll be a jester in a king's court. And your fame will draw people from far and near. They'll come to hear your jokes and learn from your cleverness."

"Thank you, O killer of demons," said Rama humbly, for he was enough in control to realize that as curses go this was a mild one. "I am most grateful."

As the goddess vanished in a flash of light, Tenali Rama went home to break the news to his waiting parents that Kali herself had found him a career.

Kali's Curse

Notes on
Kali's Curse

Tenali Rama (sometimes called Tenali Ramakrishna) is another of those historical figures around whom legends have grown. He lived in the ninth century A.D. Perhaps the goddess Kali's curse was really a blessing, because Tenali Rama grew to be a combination of wise man and jester in the court of King Krishna Deva Raya, who ruled a kingdom called Vijayanagar in the south-central part of the subcontinent. To the king Tenali Rama meted out wisdom and humor in equal doses, and passed into the legend of southern India.

My father has a supply of Tenali Rama stories which he airs as the occasion demands. This particular one highlights Rama's wit, but also shows us a joking, familiar relationship between a mortal and a goddess. Somewhere beneath her fearsome exterior, this goddess has a funny bone!

Note how the palindrome works in Sanskrit. In English, vowels and consonants are separate letters. In the Sanskrit script (used today in Indian languages like Hindi) vowel strokes are attached to consonants to form combined sounds.

A.K. Ramanujan's collection, *Folktales from India: A Selection of Oral Tales from Twenty-two Languages* (New York: Pantheon, 1988), features a few Tenali Rama tales, including this one. His notes mention a variant of this story in which the goddess gets angry because she offers Rama two pots, one containing wit and the other wisdom, and asks him to choose. Instead he grabs both pots and drinks up the contents.

Supriya's Bowl

Hard times starve people's spirits as well as their bodies. So it was once, when the Buddha lived and famine struck the land. The rains failed, and the heat of the sun withered the harvest in the field. River beds turned to dirt tracks carved into hard, dry soil. All around, in villages and towns, the cries of pain and hunger could be heard.

In the midst of this misery, some people grew greedy and selfish. The Buddha's followers came to him, bringing stories of sadness and shame.

"One merchant in town stabbed another," said one, "and all for a bag of grain."

"I heard of a woman who sold her last goat to buy some flour. On her way home she was attacked by robbers, and the flour was stolen," said another.

"Saddest of all, Lord Buddha," said a third, "are the stories of children dying of hunger on the poor side of town, because the wealthy have hoarded all the grain and milk and sugar."

"Call all the people together," said the Buddha. "Let us see what we can do to help those who cannot help themselves."

So the Buddha's followers called a big meeting. Hundreds of people came. Rich and poor, well fed and starving, dressed in silks and rags—out of respect for the Buddha and his teachings, they came to hear his words.

108

Supriya's Bowl

The Buddha said, "Citizens of this fair land, surely there is enough food in the storehouses of the wealthy to feed everyone. If the rich share what they have in the lean season, then you will all survive to enjoy the benefits of the next good harvest."

The poor and the hungry looked hopeful at the Buddha's words, but the rich people grumbled, and began offering excuses.

"My granary is empty," lied one.

"This is a big town, and the poor are lazy. Let them work for me and I will pay them as they deserve," said another. "Then they can use the money to buy the food I have stored."

"There are too many poor people," said a third. "Let them go somewhere else."

The Buddha looked around. He sighed when his eye fell upon the hard faces of people with hearts of stone. "Is there no one here," he asked finally, "who will take on the job of helping to feed the poor and homeless in these hard times?"

There was silence. Then a small voice piped up, "I will, Lord Buddha."

Out of the crowd stepped a girl, no more than six or seven years old. She was a merchant's child, dressed in fine silk. She wore tiny gold earrings. Flowers were braided in her hair.

"My name is Supriya," said the child, "and I have a bowl, to fill with food for the hungry. When can I begin?"

The Buddha smiled. "Small child," he said, "your heart is filled with love, but how will you do this alone? Your bowl is empty."

Supriya replied, "Not alone, Lord Buddha, but with your help. I'll take this bowl from house to house, and ask for food for the poor and homeless. It will not be refused. I know it."

Looking at the child, with her earnest face and shining eyes, even

Supriya's Bowl

the most selfish among those present grew ashamed.

"I have a little grain in my storehouse," mumbled one.

"I have some pickled mango from summer's harvest," said another. "After all, without the poor to work in the fields, there would be no harvest."

"My father was poor once. I'm ashamed to have forgotten," muttered a third.

Then Supriya took her bowl and every day she went from house to house in the rich part of town. Wherever she went, little by little, the bowl got filled. Sometimes an old grandmother would fill it with rice from a kitchen. Sometimes the children of a house would give up their sweets for the day. Often, others would join Supriya with their bowls, and help her take the food to the people who needed it. And sometimes, it is said, when the day was long and Supriya was tired of walking, she would sit and rest in the shade of a banyan tree. When she awoke, she would find the bowl had magically filled itself.

"Now," said Supriya, "the hungry will eat, and the people of this town will take care of each other." And so they did.

Notes on
Supriya's Bowl

The story of Supriya and her bowl, with its messages of compassion, social justice, and the power of community, surely holds meaning for our time. Supriya's story is told in Buddhist texts dating back to the seventh century B.C., that were originally written in the Pali language. Many Buddhist texts were written in this common tongue, rather than Sanskrit, which was seen as the language of the elite in Hindu society.

When people are ignorant and persist in clinging to earthly goods and attachments, Buddhism holds that suffering is the result. The rich people in this story clung to their hoarded food and would not give it up. It took the young child Supriya's compassionate words to open their eyes and their hearts.

Women Saints, East and West edited by Swami Ghanananda, is a collection of stories about the lives of women in religion, and includes a retelling of this story (Hollywood, CA: Vedanta Press, 1979).

Pronunciation Guide

Many of the character names and italicized words in these stories come from Sanskrit. A few are from languages spoken in India today, such as Dogri (as in the story, *The Goddess and the Girl)*, and Tamil (as in the story, *The Mother of Karaikkal)*. The following are some general rules for Sanskrit pronunciation:

The letter *a* in Sanskrit is sometimes pronounced long, as in *father*. Sometimes it is pronounced like a short *u*, as in *but*. (See *Satya-van*, where the first a and the second are short, but the third is long.)

The letter e is pronounced like an English *ay*, as in *bay*. (See Adisesha)

The letter *i* is pronounced like *ee* as in *meet*. (See Sita)

The letter *o* is close to an English *o* as in *ghost*. (See Gotami)

The letter *u* is pronounced *oo* as in *foot* (e.g. Supriya)

The letters *ri* are considered one letter in Sanskrit, and that letter is a vowel. Pronounce it like the *ri* in *river*, but with a very short *i* sound. (See *Ri*shi).

The letter *g* is usually hard, as in *go* (e.g. Ganga, Gotami)

The letter *d* is sometimes a hard *d*, as in *day*, sometimes a softer *th*, closest to the sound in *this*. (See *D*urga). This rule holds for the *d* in Baz Baha*d*ur, even though that name is Muslim and therefore has origins different from those of Hindu and Buddhist names.

Pronunciation Guide

The letter *t* is pronounced with a soft sound, somewhat like a *t* in the Spanish *tortilla*.

Some consonants with an *h* after them are pronounced in a special way: *jh*, similar to the combined sounds in brid*ge h*and, (see *Jh*ansi); *bh* as in a*bh*or (see Maha*bh*arata). The letters *ddh*, as in Buddha, are sounded like a soft *d* together with a *dh* as in child-*h*ood, a combination for which there is no English equivalent.

Finally, in Sanskrit, as in many Indian languages, all syllables of a word receive equal emphasis.

A List of Characters

 Adisesha (Aa-thee-say-shuh): Hooded serpent on whose coils Vishnu sleeps.

Agastya (Uh-gusth-yuh): Rishi who put the Vindhya Mountains in their place.

Ananda (Aa-nun-thuh): The Buddha's disciple.

Andal (Aan-daall): She who rules the Lord. Name of eighth century woman poet.

Arjuna (Uhr-joo-nuh): Warrior whose chariot Krishna drove in the *Mahabharata*.

Baz Bahadur (Baaz Buh-haa-thoor): Fifteenth century ruler of state of Malwa.

Bharat Mata (Bhaa-ruth Maa-thaa): Mother India (Hindi).

Bhishma (Bheesh-muh): Son of the river goddess Ganga.

Bhoomi (Bhoo-mee): The earth goddess. Also known as Bhoomidevi (Bhoo-mee-thay-vee), Bhoodevi (Bhoo-thay-vee).

Brahma (Bruh-muh): A god, creator of the universe.

Chitrangada (Chith-run-guh-thaa): A princess, minor character in one of the branch stories of the *Mahabharata*.

Dasharatha (Thuh-shuh-ruh-thuh): A king, father of prince Ram.

Devaki (Thay-vuh-kee): Birth mother of the cowherd god Krishna.

A List of Characters

Draupadi (Thrau-puh-thee): Mother of Arjuna and his brothers, the Pandavas. A character in the Mahabharata.

Buddha (Bood-thuh): The enlightened one. Founder of the Buddhist faith. Note that in this word, the letter *u* in Sanskrit is pronounced with a short *oo* sound as in *foot*, rather than the longer sound that is used in the common Western pronunciation of the word.

Durga (Thoor-gah): A fierce goddess created from the combined energies of Brahma, Vishnu, and Shiva.

Ganga (Gun-gaa): River goddess.

Gotami (Goh-thuh-mee): A Buddhist nun, follower of the Buddha.

Indra (In-thruh): King of the gods.

Janaka (Juh-nuh-kuh): King of Mithila, foster father of Sita.

Jatayu (Juh-taa-yoo): Vulture king who battled the demon Ravana in the *Ramayana*.

Kali (Kaa-lee): Vengeful mother goddess, incarnation of Parvati.

Kamsa (Kum-suh): Villainous king whose destruction was one reason for Krishna's coming to earth.

Karaikkal Amma/Ammaiyar (Kaa-ry-kull Um-maa/Um-my-yar): In Tamil, the mother of Karaikkal.

Kaurava (Kow-ruh-vuh): Rival clan who fought the Pandavas in the *Mahabharata*.

Kodai (Koh-thy): Another name for Andal.

Krishna (Krish-nuh): Cowherd god, incarnation of Vishnu.

A List of Characters

Krishna Deva Raya (Krish-nuh Thay-vuh Raa-yuh): Ninth century ruler in south-central India.

Kunti (Koon-thee): Mother of the Pandavas. A character in the Mahabharata.

Lakshmana (Luksh-muh-nuh): Brother of the hero prince Rama.

Lakshmi (Luksh-mee): Goddess of wealth.

Lakshmibai (Luksh-mee-bye): Nineteenth century queen who defied British rule in India.

Mahamaya (Muh-haa-maa-yaa): "Great Illusion," another name and form for the goddess.

Mahisha (Muh-hee-shuh): Water buffalo; a name for the demon killed by the goddess Durga.

Manmatha (Mun-muh-thuh): The god of love, usually shown as a handsome young man.

Manu (Muh-noo): Childhood name for Lakshmibai, the queen of Jhansi.

Maricha (Maa-ree-chuh): A demon, Ravana's uncle in the *Ramayana*.

Maya (Maa-yaa): The Buddha's mother.

Moropant (Moh-roh-punth): Father of the queen of Jhansi.

Nanda (Nun-thuh): A cowherd, foster father of the god Krishna.

Narada (Naa-ruh-thuh): A *rishi* who wanders through the worlds (sometimes coming from the star cluster called the Pleiades), taking news place to place. A *narada* in everyday conversation is one who carries tales.

A List of Characters

Pajapati (Puh-jaa-puh-thee): The Buddha's stepmother, second queen of his father. Sometimes called Prajapati (Pruh-jaa-puh-thee).

Pandava (Paan-duh-vuh): A son of Pandu. Arjuna was a Pandava.

Pandu (Paan-doo): A king, whose sons fought the battle that forms the heart of the story of the *Mahabharata*.

Parvati (Paar-vuh-thee): A goddess, companion to Shiva.

Rama (Raa-muh): The hero prince whose story is one of the epics of Hindu mythology. Incarnation of Vishnu.

Rati (Ruh-thee): Goddess of love, consort of Manmatha.

Ravana (Raa-vuh-nuh): The ten-headed demon who is the villain in the story of the *Ramayana*.

Rewa (Ray-vaa): A river goddess.

Roopmati (Roop-muh-thee): A princess of the kingdom of Mandu, in the present-day Indian state of Rajasthan.

Saraswati (Suh-rus-vuh-thee): The goddess of learning.

Satyavan (Suth-yuh-vaan): A prince, Savitri's husband.

Savitri (Saa-vith-ree): A princess, Satyavan's wife.

Shankara (Shun-kuh-ruh): A Hindu reformer of the eighth century A.D.

Shantanu (Shaan-thuh-noo): A king who married the river goddess Ganga.

Supriya (Soo-pree-yaa): The little girl whose compassion saved the poor from starvation.

A List of Characters

Shiva (Shi-vuh): God of destruction or dissolution.

Siddhartha (Sid-dhar-thuh): The prince who, upon attaining enlightenment, became the Buddha.

Sita (See-thaa): The princess who is the heroine of the *Ramayana*, incarnation of the goddess Lakshmi.

Sri (Shree): Another name for the goddess Lakshmi. Also Sridevi (Shree-thay-vee).

Tenali Rama (Then-aa-lee Raa-muh): A ninth century A.D. jester, from the village of Tenali.

Uma (Oo-maa): Another name for Parvati.

Vaishno Devi (Vie-shno Thay-vee): The goddess of a famous northern shrine, in the Jammu region of the present Indian state of Jammu and Kashmir.

Vak (Vaak): In the *Vedas*, the goddess of speech. No stories of her survive in the Hindu mythology of today.

Valmiki (Vaal-mee-kee): A blind poet, said to have written the best-known version of the *Ramayana*.

Vashishtha (Vuh-shish-tuh): A *rishi.*

Vasudeva (Vaa-soo-thay-vuh): A nobleman, mortal father to the god Krishna.

Vindhyavasini (Vin-dhyaa-vaa-si-nee): She who lives in the Vindhya Mountains. A form of the goddess.

Vishnu (Vish-noo): God who preserves order in the universe.

A List of Characters

Vishnu Sharma (Vish-noo Shuhr-muh): Legendary writer of the *Panchatantra*, one of the world's earliest story collections.

Vishnuchitta (Vish-noo-chit-thuh): An eighth century priest and scholar, foster father of the poet Andal.

Yama (Yuh-muh): God of death.

Yashoda (Yuh-show-daa): Wife of a cowherd, foster mother of the god Krishna.

Glossary

Amma (Um-maa): Mother

Angrez (Ung-rayz): The British (Hindi). Possibly a corruption of the word "English." The English language is called Angrezi (Ung-ray-zee).

Asura (Uh-soo-ruh): A demon.

Bhakti (Bhuk-thee): Literally, faith. Name of tradition of worship and poetry dating back to about the eighth century A.D.

Deva (Thay-vuh): A god.

Devi (Thay-vee): Name for the goddess in her many forms.

Gayatri Mantra (Gaa-yuh-three Mun-thra): A Hindu chant.

Jataka (Jaa-tuh-kuh): A story of a life of the Buddha, in one of various human and animal forms.

Mahabharata (Muh-haa-bhaa-ruh-thuh): One of the two epic stories of Hindu mythology.

Mantra (Mun-thruh): A chant or verse, sometimes said to carry special powers.

Panchatantra (Pun-chuh-thun-thruh): Ancient story collection.

Purana (Poo-raa-nuh): Ancient Hindu text.

Rakshasa (Raak-shuh-suh): A demon; fem. Rakshasi (Raak-shuh-see).

Glossary

Ramayana (Raa-maa-yuh-nuh): One of the two epic stories of Hindu mythology.

Rani (Raa-nee): A queen.

Rishi (Ri-shee): Holy man or saint who has renounced the world.

Sangha (Sun-ghuh): Buddhist holy order.

Shakti (Shuk-thee): Strength or power, seen as a trait of the goddess.

Tanpura (Thaan-poo-ruh): A four-stringed drone instrument.

Tulasi (Thoo-luh-see): The holy basil plant, used in Hindu worship and in traditional medicine.

Veda (Vay-thuh): Sacred Hindu text said to have been composed by the sage Vyasa. There are four *Vedas*.

Source Notes

Source information for each story, oral or previously written, is contained in the note following the story. Permission was obtained as indicated for reprint or adaptation of previously published material:

The verse from the Therigatha used as an epigraph is reprinted by permission of The Feminist Press at the City University of New York, from *Women Writing in India: Volume I: 600 B.C. to the Early Twentieth Century*, edited by Susie Tharu and K. Lalita. Compilation © 1991 Susie Tharu and K. Lalita.

"The Buddha and the Five Hundred Queens" is adapted from *Myths of the Hindus and Buddhists* by Ananda K. Coomaraswamy and Sister Nivedita. New York: Dover Publications, 1967. Adaptation is by permission of the publisher and Dr. R.P. Coomaraswamy, executor of the first author's estate.

"The Mother of Karaikkal" is adapted from *Slaves of the Lord: The Path of the Tamil Saints,* by Vidya Dehejia (New Delhi: Munshiram Manoharlal, 1988). Adaptation is by permission of the author.

"The Daughter-in-Law Who Got Her Way" is adapted from *Folktales from India: A Selection of Oral Tales from Twenty-two Languages*, selected and retold by A.K. Ramanujan (New York: Pantheon, 1988). Adaptation is by permission of Pantheon Books, a division of Random House, Inc.

"Gotami and the Mustard Seed" is adapted from a variant of the tale in Mabel Bode, "Women Leaders of the Buddhist Reformation,"

Source Notes

Journal of the Royal Asiatic Society of Great Britain and Ireland, 1893: 793-96.

"Supriya's Bowl" is adapted from *Women Saints, East and West* edited by Swami Ghanananda (Hollywood, CA: Vedanta Press, 1979). Adaptation is by permission of the publisher.

"Sita's Story" is based on ideas found in women's retellings of the *Ramayana*, and on Madhu Kishwar's article, "Yes to Sita, No to Ram! The Continuing Popularity of Sita in India" in *Manushi*, 98: January-February 1997. Selected portions of the article are adapted by permission of the author.

Acknowledgments

My thanks to the American Association of University Women for the grant that began all this, and special thanks to Terry Sayler. To Emily Ferren, Pat Rinehart, and Susan Frank, for their kindness and hospitality. To children in Garrett and Caroline counties, Maryland, for listening, writing, and asking thoughtful and important questions.

To the goddess—who else could have overseen two moves and a book within a year? To Diantha, in the hope she'll keep the lamp burning.

To my mother, Vasantha Krishnaswami, who cheerfully abandoned vacation plans to accommodate my quest for stories. To R. Gopalaswamy and Subhashini Bose, for helping me check my facts.

To Sumant and Nikhil Krishnaswamy, of course.

To Swami Brahmarupananda, of the Chinmaya Mission, Silver Spring, Maryland, and to Lee-Ellen Marvin, who read my manuscript and offered ideas and encouragement. To Vilasini Balakrishnan, for books, tapes, and *chai.* To Shanti Mahajan, for the kid point of view.

To Elisa Carbone, Sally Davies, Mary Ella Randall, and Mary Templet, for friendship and criticism in perfect proportion.

And that's the short list!